KNOWING ONE'S PLACE

After thirty years of marriage, Beth Crome has started to question what the future holds - and even whether she is married to the right man. She and Sam have been happy enough together, but life seems suddenly very empty.

On a whim Beth jets off to visit her children in New York and Hong Kong. All this is exciting and stimulating at first, but gradually Beth begins to miss Sam, and to appreciate the value of true love.

KNOWING ONE'S PLACE

Francis Paige titles available from
Severn House Large Print

Bid Time Return
A Day at the Races
Game to Miss Cowan
The Summer Fields

KNOWING ONE'S PLACE

Frances Paige

Severn House Large Print
London & New York

This first large print edition published in Great Britain 2004 by
SEVERN HOUSE LARGE PRINT BOOKS LTD of
9-15 High Street, Sutton, Surrey, SM1 1DF.
First world regular print edition published 2004 by
Severn House Publishers, London and New York.
This first large print edition published in the USA 2004 by
SEVERN HOUSE PUBLISHERS INC., of
595 Madison Avenue, New York, NY 10022.

British Library Cataloguing in Publication Data

Paige, Frances
    Knowing one's place. - Large print ed.
    1.   Midlife crisis - Fiction
    2.   Separation (Psychology) - Fiction
    3.   Marriage - Fiction
    4.   Love stories
    5.   Large type books
    I.   Title
    823.9'14 [F]

ISBN 0-7278-7387-3

Printed and bound in Great Britain by
MPG Books Ltd, Bodmin, Cornwall.

For Helen

One

1976

It took Beth Crome a long time before she realized she was married to the wrong man – about thirty years to be exact. It happened in the Palmintes Park in Gran Canaria, when she stood with Sam, her husband, and watched two lovebirds loving each other.

'Aren't they sweet?' The phrase echoed all around her, as cloying as honey. She recognized German, Spanish, French.

Sam was busy taking photographs. He photographed everything that moved, or rather he waited *until* it moved, then pressed the shutter. He had no eye, and so the photographs were always fuzzy and ill-judged.

But as she stood and looked – she felt her chilblains burning; it was peculiar that on this island of sunshine she should still have the chilblains that had plagued her all winter in dreary England, the doctor had said she was run down – she realized that the lovebirds, were not loving at all. They were performing a mutual service. It was a symbiotic relationship – a searching with their beaks for mites in each other's feathers.

And, she went on to think, standing there in the hot sunshine with her chilblains flaming, who am I to say that I married the wrong man? What is so bloody right about *me?*

'Damn!' husband Sam said at her side. 'They've moved again, the little buggers!'

'They saw you coming,' she said. 'Never mind, there are plenty more where they came from.' A truism, to say the least, in this two-hundred-thousand square metres of subtropical oasis with its springs and lakes and its thousands of palms and its one hundred and fifty thousand exotic birds, of which more than five hundred flew freely in the park. 'A Photo Paradise', the brochure claimed. Cockerels, cockatoos and toucans; balefully beaked, Schiaperelli-pink flamingos with arthritically jointed stick legs; hummingbirds – mere brilliant flashes – and peacocks, the most macho birds in the world, she thought as she and Sam wandered amongst the agave forests and the aloe forests, and the palms which occasionally gave a leathery rustle in the breeze. You scratch my back and I'll scratch yours. I'll go out and work and you'll have the babies. And in this New Age they were living in, those roles were sometimes exchanged – the female going out to work having dropped her young, so to speak, in the nest, leaving them to be minded and fed by the male. Who sometimes proved to be better at looking after the babies than his spouse, and who was happy to take the children to nursery school and collect them at the end of the day.

Once, when Sam was temporarily 'resting', i.e. out of work – he had tried various jobs before he settled down in the shop when his father died – he had filled a recipe book for Beth with tips he had garnered from the mothers in the kiddies' cloakroom. He was better at fraternizing than Beth. But he knew the rules. He never tried out the recipes himself, knew where the line was drawn, considering himself too macho to wear an apron. This was, of course, before the time men boasted about being good in the kitchen – indeed they now knew a couple at home who actually had two cookers, a His and Hers.

When they got back home from their Gran Canaria idyll, he would renew his usual activities – showing his muzzy photographs to all who would look at them, telephoning his financial adviser daily to ask if he had seen 'that bit in the FT about Lesser Holdings Incorporated' (he was concerned about his pension), going to the supermarket to see if there were any wine bargains, calling in at the shop to check on the staff, perhaps having a coffee with them, doing his crossword when he got home and having another coffee with her, going out in the evening to numerous committee meetings, driving Mrs Cochrane, their elderly next-door neighbour, to her various medical appointments (she had realized quickly that Sam's retirement meant a free taxi into town) and generally leading the life of Riley of the comfortably retired.

They had both retired at fifty-five – not retarded as yet, thank God, she thought, hanging in there. They would hardly have known they were of that class, except that they noticed beggars didn't beg from them, recognizing perhaps that here was a different kind of deprivation, the loss of youth. The ageing process, the descent into hell, the banality of it, Beth would think, exchanging silly jokes about it with dinner guests. 'Losing one's marbles'. 'Falling off the bough'. 'Past the sell-by date'. 'Gone for a burton'. Who was this Burton? *The Guardian* newspaper was there to answer such abstruse questions, or better still, get their clever readers to answer for them – that sounded to her like one of Sam's remarks, as he flicked his *Daily Telegraph*.

Beth's lovebird theory was not new, she realized. Her friend, Mary Cass, had once said to her, jokingly, that 'jokes are the things you have to watch, not the serious statements of friends'. Then she had refuted her conclusion by adding seriously, 'How could you have married a man whose politics are so different from yours?'

She had thought over Mary's remark in her insomniac hours, and found that the answer was simple. When you are lusting after each other morning, noon and night, politics is the last thing you think about. Sam could have been a Trotskyite for all she cared. Her mind would drift back to those youthful days, pictures of that early domestic bliss would float before her eyes. The frolicking in bed which had resulted in Laurel and Nicholas, and would have resulted in many more had they not decided to fight nature with the means which the New Age had provided, and limit their family to the national average of two and a half children. They disregarded the half.

There was the remembered joy of hanging over the side of the cot, marvelling at what they had produced. Laurel in her frilled cot, the little mouth like a peeled leaf of a blood orange, lashes lying on her flushed cheeks, the curled, crumpled fists – those curled, crumpled fists were the only part which looked slightly unfinished, made the tears spurt from her eyes. And before that, Nicholas in a more masculine variation, a broader forehead, the small chin between the apple cheeks, the masculine look, even at such an early age.

Well, it had been worth it, the decision to give up a good job for five years, thereby missing promotion over that traitor, Lawson, who had urged her to do so, but why fuss? It had been a precious time in her life.

She remembered one afternoon when she had adjusted the cover carefully round a little shoulder, an apology for a shoulder, dropped a feather kiss on the broad forehead, two thirds of a forehead to one third of a face – it must have been Nicholas – and tiptoed into the kitchen. She had started to make a cup of tea, put her feet up and read that book of Sam Bellow's she had bought to keep her brain working.

Mid-kettle, she heard the noise of a car stopping in the drive. Or was it a van? But van drivers didn't usually drive up drives.

The key in the door. Had Sam got the push, been in an accident? – he wouldn't be putting his key in the door in that case. 'Hello, Beth!' She had heard his voice, cheerful, energetic, the voice of an extrovert man, as was his laugh, and there he was, blue-suited, fresh and young, university tie. 'Darling!' he said loudly. An extrovert voice.

'Shush,' she had said, holding up a hand. 'I've just settled him down. Why are you home at this time? Are you all right?'

'Am I all right? Am I *all right?*' His vocabulary wasn't large. 'No, I missed lunch. Got to thinking about you. I was desperate for you. Raines in the office asked if I was going to have a bite of lunch, and I said no, I had forgotten something, I'd drive home and get it. *Get* it, darling,' he said, leering.

'Have a cup of tea first,' she suggested, smiling at this boy whom she had married.

'No, I haven't time for both.' He was drawing her out of her chair, putting his arms round her, drawing her close, close, his arms slipping down her back, low down so that she could feel how needy he was. 'Come upstairs,' he said, 'or I'll have you on the floor!'

'I don't mind.' Her vocal chords were always affected by desire, resulting in a blackbird-like croak. Her memories swirled like a Catherine wheel in her head. Cold tiles. 'Remember Nicholas, sleeping...' Fumbling, sweating, groaning, ecstasy, the croaky joyous giggling at the end. Sam blue-suited again and in his right mind, munching at a doughnut and noisily drinking tea. 'See you tonight!'

Oh, that part had been all right. It had blotted out everything else, most of all her thought processes, the fine-tuning of her mind, her critical faculties. Well, it had all been worth it, her decision when she became pregnant again to give up that interesting publishing job for five years, thereby missing promotion over that sewer rat, Lawson.

The Lawsons hadn't any children, and she had bonded with hers so strongly that it would have taken a solvent to unglue them. *Had* she, she wondered now? Nicholas had dropped out of university and gone to Hong Kong, and Laurel had begged to go to

London, and had run into trouble there.

Sam had persuaded her to let her go, and she had agreed, thinking that there was a bonus to it – daughter in London, son in Hong Kong – and she would be free from the endless bickering with Laurel. 'Other girls' mothers let them...' The peer argument which every parent recognizes.

But here they were in the Seventies. Laurel had, after her disastrous sortie to London, gone to visit Nicholas in Hong Kong – that had been Sam's idea – and met an American, Jake Stansby, who had come back with her to be introduced and to declare their intention to get married. Then there had been the invitation to Sam and Beth from his parents to visit them at their summer home in Long Island.

They had accepted the invitation and found the parents installed in a place called Sag Harbour. Judging by the set-up there, the New York house must be something, Sam said. The Stansbys had said how much they loved Laurel already, and seemed only too willing to welcome her into the bosom of their family. There seemed to be a lot of

Stansbys. Two 'kids', as they were affection-
ally called by their parents, Betsy and
Maybelle, and two daughters of the father's
first marriage, Nancy and Claire, who
worked in New York, and, of course, Jake,
their brother. They only met Nancy, who
was on holiday at the time, but the whole of
the Stansby family struck Sam and Beth as
welcoming, and more than suitable, judging
by their style and influence. To put it
crudely, although neither Sam nor Beth did
so, Laurel had fallen on her feet.

Bob Stansby, who was the provider of all
the luxury that surrounded them, had a
publishing house in New York, trade magazines only, which gave him and Beth a
common topic, although she judged that the
firm he owned could have swallowed up the
one she had worked for in one gulp.

Joanne Stansby had asked one favour from
them – could she and her two step-daugh-
ters, Nancy and Claire, be allowed to plan
the wedding? And would they agree to it
being held in Riverdale, their house near
New York? She realized she was taking away
this privilege from Laurel's parents, but of

course Sam and Beth must come and stay at Broadacres, the Riverdale house.

They both realized that they were being swept away by the generosity and charm of the Stansbys, but gave in gracefully. Sam said he could always take photographs to show to their friends, but Beth reckoned there would surely be a vellum-bound album. And those friends who were curious and had money to spare could be invited.

The wedding had been a great success. Laurel had looked lovely and happy in her white satin gown, flanked by her two sisters-in-law-to-be in pale green chiffon, and the little ones were in the same colour, carrying baskets of primroses. Laurel looked virginal with white lilies, regal and different from the harum-scarum girl they had known, as if she was fulfilling her role as a member of the Stansby family. Jake looked suitably adoring and handsome, and seemed to be correspondingly adored by the large crowd of well-wishers.

They met a lot of smart New York people, who made them feel ten-feet tall as the parents of the bride, admired again the signs of wealth in the Riverdale house, and returned home to their more modest establishment in the Lakes with Sam's photographs showing the extensive grounds of Broadacres and views of the house, which he passed around guests at dinner parties. The expression of their friends' faces saved them extolling the virtues of the Stansbys.

Beth had been so exhausted by all this excitement that they had gone to Gran Canaria to recuperate, and let their feet touch ground.

Nicholas had been a worry at first when he had dropped out of university and got a job with a travel agency in Hong Kong, but quickly made his way, flying all over the world, fixing up hotels and holidays for his firm, and buying an expensive flat overlooking the port. Privately, Beth thought it was because he was so personable that his firm had recognized he was right for the job. He had never quite fitted in with his friends in the Lakes. She thought his style was more London than Wetherham, and Sam was more impressed with Nicholas's ability in rock climbing, but would have liked him to be more like he'd been in his youth – a bit of a tearaway with girls. Nicholas had always had a slightly supercilious air, unlike Laurel, who fraternized more easily.

Nicholas had flown to New York for the wedding, and had been charming to Laurel's sisters-in-law, Nancy and Claire, and their friends, who called him Nick. Beth had always disliked the abbreviation, and never used it. The phrase 'Chris and I' appeared in his letters home a lot, but he didn't divulge much about his life in Hong Kong. Nor did he invite Sam and Beth to visit them. They had spent all their savings on Laurel's wedding and travel, so they hadn't so far done so. Besides, they had seen him at the wedding, and Sam felt he had to get Beth away for a holiday so that she could relax.

When the children had been younger, Beth had always thought of Nicholas as her favourite, more like her, and indeed there had been a good rapport between them. Perhaps that was why Sam favoured Laurel, who had his open, friendly nature. Beth had thought when she saw Nicholas at the wedding that he looked as handsome as ever in his fairness, but that he was developing a double chin, and his blue eyes had acquired a steely glint.

'Do you think he's gay?' she had asked Sam afterwards, and he had looked surprised, said it had never occurred to him. He had thought that when he spoke of Chris, it was short for Christine. Or Christopher, she had thought. Perhaps he had been trying to tell them something. Time would tell, she said.

On their way back from Gran Canaria, Beth had spent the four-hour flight to London reviewing the conclusion she had arrived at in Palmintes Park – that their marriage had come to an end. They had reared two satisfactory children, one married, the other probably gay – but that was typical of the times they lived in – and now she and Sam were thrown together.

And there was the sex. A few months ago Sam had declared himself 'not interested', as if, now that they had retired, his duties were over. They had produced their quota of children, and they could sit back. And yet she saw him at parties being charming to the women there, and seeming to enjoy their company. Was the fault hers?

She had asked him that, but he had looked away and said he would rather not talk about it. The feeling of rejection had been strong. 'What is your problem, Sam?' she had asked him, very reasonably, one morning. 'Shouldn't you see a doctor?' But he had buried himself in his crossword and told her not to be silly. 'You're always analysing things, Beth. Leave it alone.'

She remembered how at Laurel's wedding he had charmed the American ladies, and how quite a few of them had told her how delightful he was, which had made her examine herself. Had Sam been right? Was there something off-putting about her? She noticed how the American ladies fussed over him, larded him with compliments, listened to his opinions as if they were words of wisdom, while to her analytical mind they seemed to be tosh. Was it that these women, mostly in their fifties, had come to the conclusion that to have a happy marriage, you had to make a man feel good about himself? Now that the sex they had enjoyed had dropped away like a cloak, leaving her feeling naked, she had to ask herself if that was all that had held them together. She remembered long car journeys when they didn't have anything to say to each other, as if they were inhibited, and yet neither of them was so tongue-tied with other people.

I'll have a down-to-earth talk with him when we get home, she promised herself. She would say that something seemed to have gone out of their marriage, and that she'd been contemplating some radical changes, such as going off somewhere to think it all over. Then there was always the possibility of going back to work, although she hated the thought of being in competition with young girls in whatever job she found.

'Soon be back home,' Sam said, folding his newspaper beside her on the plane.

'Yes.' She too had heard the captain's announcement that they would be arriving at Heathrow in five minutes. She shut her book.

'At least I haven't as much grass to cut as the Stansbys.'

There didn't seem to be anything to say to that, except, 'Surely the extent of the lawns at Riverdale haven't been rankling all that time.' Or, 'Don't forget Bob Stansby can afford a live-in gardener.' Which sounded acerbic, she knew. And Sam was quite right. It was home.

And so, after the flurry at the airport, waiting for their cases – always last, it seemed – getting a taxi home, and finding the house quite unchanged but looking strange and neglected, although tidy. No ticking of the grandfather clock in the hall, Sam's job. No flowers, her job. She got her car out and drove to the supermarket to get provisions for a meal – she had suggested going out, but Sam had been busy with his mail and didn't want to go, and now they were sitting at one end of the dining table, across from each other, the other end taken up by torn envelopes, piles of brochures, magazines and letters.

'I had such a time at Sainsbury's,' she said. 'The vegetables! I had to search for decent salad stuff, and meat, I had to take chops...'

'Why didn't you buy two of those ready-made jobs? Mary Cass tells me she lives on them.'

'Mary Cass is a widow. She has only herself to think about.'

'She says she quite enjoys being a widow.'

'Does she? I don't want to talk about Mary Cass. Sam.' She put down her knife and fork. 'Do you like being married?'

'Well, I've never complained.' He looked up at her, smiling. 'It's been going on for a long time.'

'Don't you get the feeling we've reached some sort of *impasse*? People talk about what fun it is when you retire. I haven't felt that. I don't even feel you love me any more.' This wasn't how she wanted it to go, and she disliked the idea of appealing like that to her husband.

'You're tired with the journey. You know what Alan said. What you need is a good sleep.' He attacked his lamb chop.

'I'm not particularly tired, but I got a feeling of hopelessness when I came through the door. Sort of, "Here we go again".'

'Hasn't the holiday done you good? That was why we went, if you remember. Doctor's orders. To recover from the last year, New York and everything.'

'No, it's made me see things more clearly. Life stretching ahead with you and me here, following our usual pattern, and I get this feeling of hopelessness.'

'Once you get into the swing of things, your friends, your keep-fit, and so on...'

'There's something missing...'

He looked at her. 'Are you trying to tell me that the status quo doesn't suit you?'

'Well, when we both retired, I thought we would have things to do together, to talk about, but that hasn't happened.'

'We've just had a holiday, and before that we were in America...'

'Yes, I know, but it's the status quo...'

'I'm sorry. I looked at it in a different way. I thought you would have more time for your own interests, and so should I...'

She remembered how she had planned to take weekend courses, go to lectures, the opera at Manchester. 'We never seem to have anything to talk about.'

'Do you know why that is?'

'No.'

'You despise me. I've always felt it.' He looked at her over his paper and his eyes were sad. It was like a blow to her chest, but she rallied.

'What rubbish! Despise you? Who's been filling up your head with that rubbish? It couldn't be Mary Cass, could it?'

'No, it isn't Mary Cass, but I sometimes wish you were as easy and relaxed as she is. I know you don't think much of her house, its untidiness, but it's a house you can drop into at any time...'

'Is that what you've been doing?'

'I do, sometimes. We're both interested in gardening. I take plants to her, do a bit of digging for her...'

'How cosy! And I expect you discuss me at the same time?'

'Mary's not like that.' His voice seemed to soften.

'Have you fallen in love with her? Is that why you're so uninterested in me in bed?'

He looked ashamed, and she thought he

looked like Nick during that period when he was wetting the bed and tried to hide it. She went on, 'I think we could both do with a separation if we are to save our marriage.' This was the sentence she had prepared on the plane. He didn't reply. He was looking at his chop.

'Do you agree, Sam?'

'If that's what you want. What will you tell our friends?'

'The truth.'

'It won't satisfy them.' He put down his knife and fork. 'Remember, you brought this on yourself. I have to tell you that I am attracted to Mary Cass, but she wouldn't wish to break up our marriage.'

She felt another blow, this time in her stomach. 'So that's what's wrong? Your lack of interest?'

'It's *your* lack of interest, Beth. Because of that we've grown away from each other. I had put it in the background recently because of our jaunting about. Mary is quite different. We chat away and I feel at ease with her. She's not critical. But I don't forget how fond you and I were of each other. It could never be like that with Mary. Though I realize that one's marriage has to change as one grows older – that is, allowances have to be made on both sides.' The sad eyes again. 'This wouldn't have happened if you hadn't made it abundantly clear that you despised me.'

'Don't use that word. I don't like it.'

'It's true. Oh, I've seen that look in your eyes when I start to speak! You've destroyed my confidence in myself, and when I'm alone with you, I'm aware of your eyes on me, as if you were waiting for me to make a mistake.'

'What nonsense!' And yet, was that the reason why they were so uncomfortable when they were alone together? Often at the hotel in Gran Canaria, she had looked round the dining room at other tables and seen other couples laughing together, and thought, what's wrong with us? And yet, wasn't it true that she was too critical, especially of his politics?

'Why shouldn't I have my own opinions?' he said. 'I don't agree with yours. They're so...confrontational.'

'And Mary Cass's are not.' If she's got any...Unfair, she chastised herself. 'Mary's a nice woman,' she said. 'I like her. She does a lot of good in the village. If anything wants doing, the cry goes up for Mary Cass. But, now that her name has been mentioned, are you sleeping with her?'

He met her eyes and looked down. 'There was only one night. We got tipsy and we both regretted it.'

She was surprised at the sensation she felt. Like a sword piercing her. She knew blood pulsed in her cheeks, betraying her surprise. 'Well, well,' she said, 'at least you're honest. Only one night?' She saw his bent head nod. 'Would you go and live with her if I left?'

'Hey, hey!' His head jerked upwards. 'You're always in a hurry! We've never discussed it. She would never break up a marriage.'

It was on the tip of Beth's tongue to say, 'But she has.' But she reminded herself of Palmintes Park. That *she* had made up her mind first about their marriage, and here was Sam surprising *her*, having done something about it. You're not going to be a dog in the manger, are you? she asked herself. 'Would you?' she repeated.

'I told you, we haven't discussed things like that. But since it seems that *you* want to, the sensible thing, I suppose, would be for you to have the house and I'll move out.'

She got up and went into the kitchen. Everything was blurry. She had a horrible feeling that she had just talked herself out of a marriage.

He was at her side, holding a tea towel, lifting a plate from the draining board. 'This isn't what I wanted, Beth,' he said. 'You were always the only girl in the world for me.' That's a song, she thought.

'But *you* strayed away...' She knew she was shifting the blame.

'It was nothing like what you and I had...'

'But we don't have it now.'

'We've changed. We're older.'

They were going round in circles, she thought. She hadn't changed, only grown. She had been blinkered by passion in the early years. And she hadn't recognized that what they were left with should have been good enough. Mary Cass had.

'Perhaps one marriage isn't enough,' she said, tears blurring her voice. 'One for one's youth, the other for companionship. I didn't see that.'

'I don't want to leave you,' he said. He put down the plate he was drying and took her in his arms.

'But I have to get away to think it out. I'll visit the children, move around a bit. I have some savings. You have to make up your mind about Mary.' He didn't try to meet her eyes, nor did he contradict her.

Two

Jake and Laurel were sitting up in bed on a bright Sunday morning in their apartment on 57th Street, the *New York Times* spread between them.

'I remember when I was in Sag Harbour in your parents' house,' Laurel said. 'I saw those men with papers under their arms, like this' – she made curves of her arms – 'and I thought they were all delivery men. It was only afterwards I realized how big the Sunday papers were...Oh, look,' she said, pointing. 'She's at it again.' There was a naked woman in the opposite apartment across the street, preening herself in front of a mirror.

'Why should I look when I've got this.' He pulled down the duvet and bent lovingly over her. 'She used to excite me, but no longer.'

'Don't start. You said we were going for a run in the park and then you were taking me to the Lion's Rock for lunch.'

'So I did. And breakfast in bed. You're utterly spoiled.' He got out of bed, helped by a push from Laurel.

'Did you always sleep naked, Jake?'

'*Ça dépend*, as the French say. Tea?'

'Yes, please, I haven't got used to your constant coffee yet.'

She stretched herself luxuriously while he was in the kitchen. Marvellous to have a husband like Jake, so good in bed. And the parents liked him, which was a bonus. No opposition like there was when she had gone to London. Her mind slipped back to the rainy streets, the flat, the girls, the three of them tumbling out to work, Dave...

1964

London, London, London. The words kept bursting in her brain like fireworks as she sat in the back of Dad's car on their way there. It had all worked out beautifully. Pat, a school friend, had gone to London to do journalism, and had shacked up with another girl studying at City University, called Jan. She had offered to fit Laurel into their flat. The rooms were small, and they all shared a hanging place, curtained off in the hall for their clothes. The idea didn't appeal, as she was used to her own space, but she couldn't turn down such an offer. Mother had wanted her to travel to a business college in Carlisle so that she could keep her at home, but she had appealed to her father.

'Will you speak to her, Dad? She just wants to keep me here, and the colleges in London are far better. I could put in a word with her about your loft conversion.' He had wanted to have a loft conversion, to make an office for himself. 'Mother doesn't understand. You need a place in the house too. I'll point out to her how you love your garden shed, pottering about in summer, a place of your own, and how you need a room inside as well. Most men have a study.'

Mother always talked about the papers he

left lying about the lounge from his many committees, and he brought home a lot of stuff from the shop, the sports outfitters in Wetherham, which he had inherited from his father. The name Crome was respected all over the Lakes. It gave him status.

He must have worked a miracle with Mother because here she was, speeding to London and freedom. The arrangement was that her college fees should be paid, and her allowance should cover living expenses and fares home at stated intervals. She promised she would work hard to justify this expense.

She settled in without trouble. Pat had a boyfriend, James, who often stayed overnight, which surprised Laurel at first, but she soon got used to bumping into him at night when she was going to the bathroom. Jan hadn't a boyfriend, but would give her back teeth to have one. She got desperate at intervals, and tried agencies. When she made a date at a restaurant, she would persuade Pat and Laurel to sit at a table near them and give her their opinion later. The three of them used to go into fits of laughter afterwards, discussing her date, and eventually she gave it up.

Then Laurel and Jan began going to discos, and at one of them Laurel met Dave. He was so different from the well-brought-up boys whom she had grown up with, who went off to schools where cold baths and runs over the fells were the norm, in between playing other schools at rugby, and descending at holiday time into the valleys, rampaging around on the lookout for girls to date. She fell instantly in love with Dave, his guitar, his slenderness like a willow wand, and his husky voice, and was delighted when he suggested that she came with him to his various gigs. Being recognized as Dave's girl was sufficient reward. It was a new world, a new life, which she thought spelled sophistication. All she meant by that was that it was different from the healthy life she had lived before, where there was immediate contact with the elements, the wind, and the rain. Smoky rooms and ears filled with the constant beat of music was, to her, atmospheric, and the different people she met there were exciting. They all professed to have a link with America, although most of them were Londoners, or from Liverpool, the home of the Beatles.

Pat said to her once, 'Why don't you invite Dave to sleep over?' So she did. It was a great disappointment. He looked better in his gear than naked – no muscles – and although they never had great conversations, one would have thought he had written the original sex manual. She resented being treated as a tyro, even though she was, and she'd had to screw up her courage to invite him to the flat.

'I thought you'd never ask,' he said.

'Why?' she asked.

'You're such a well-brought-up girl, although you come from the sticks. "Yes, thank you, please may I", and all that jazz.'

But she adored how he took off the rubber band that held back his hair and let it fall all over her face when they were in bed.

During this time, she noticed that Pat began to look worried, and then she announced she was going to have an abortion. Jan and Laurel went with her and brought her home. They called her, secretly, the Awful Warning. They had a drink and she was quite cheerful, but in the middle of the night they both heard her muffled sobbing. When they went into her bedroom she was moaning over and over, 'What have I done?' Laurel felt that James should have been there, but they cheered her up with hot-water bottles and cups of tea. Laurel couldn't sleep for worrying about her, but in the morning Pat's face was set, and she thanked them both.

The trouble was that James began bashing her up. Laurel noticed the bruises, and so did Jan, but Pat lied when they tackled her, saying that she had fallen or some such nonsense.

Jan became motherly around this time, and began giving Pat uplifting talks. 'Why don't you ask him about his early life?' she asked, and Pat said, 'I did once, and he bashed me.'

'Well, you be careful,' Jan said. 'He won't pay for two abortions, and if you get pregnant again he'll persuade you to marry him. You'll become a battered bride. Once a basher, always a basher.'

The atmosphere in the flat began to seem,

to Laurel, as bad as her home environment, and she suggested they should have a party to cheer them all up. James and Dave were detailed to look after the drinks, beer and wine from the corner shop, and the girls bought loads of food from the deli near them. At the last moment Laurel dashed to the corner shop for paper napkins.

At eight o'clock the girls were ready, high hairdos and minis, and Dave and James were there for the bar. At nine o'clock no one had arrived, and they were all high, forgetting they were running a party, when the doorbell rang. Laurel ran to open the door and found what seemed like an army tumbling down the basement stairs, pushing past her shouting, 'Where is it?'

The party went with a swing, with Dave playing his guitar, and only stopping when Laurel had to ask him to run out for more beer. He looked peeved, and she knew he would remind her that she owed him some money later. His attitude towards money was the only thing about him that annoyed her, because she tried to keep to her budget whereas Dave seemed to live on air and loans. But she blamed her upbringing, when she'd had a cash box, and had been encouraged to save for birthdays, new bicycles and so on.

People started drifting away around four, and others had to be winkled out of bedrooms and despatched up the basement stairs. Jan had scored with a gatecrasher who had surged in with the rest. He was called Damien. Still motherly, she said, 'I think we should all go to bed now and leave the clearing-up till tomorrow.'

James and Pat went off, and so did Jan with Damien, and Laurel said, 'Well, I'm pretty tired too,' looking pointedly at Dave.

He was lying on the sofa, smoking, a glass of wine in his hand, and as she passed him, he raised his glass and said, 'See you.' She went to her room and fell asleep almost immediately.

At about five thirty, she wakened to the sound of voices and the smell of smoke. She went into the hall and found Jan and Damien there.

'The sitting room's full of smoke,' Damien said. He annoyed her, just standing there.

'Is it? Then we'd better get out!' She could hardly speak for coughing. 'Where's James and Pat?' Feeling suddenly terrified, she said, 'Where's Dave?'

James and Pat appeared at that moment. He had his arm round Pat. 'Where's the fire?' he was yelling. 'Pat woke me up coughing.'

'It's in the lounge,' Laurel pointed. 'Oh, James, I left Dave there. He didn't come to bed.'

'He's probably gone home,' he said, which she took as an insult.

'I don't think so. I'll just look in.' She was trying to think. Had she seen Dave in the lounge when she went to bed? It was very difficult. Her head was full of smoke.

'Don't do that!' James said. 'It could be an inferno in there.'

'It won't take a minute. On you lot go!' The four moved off and huddled together down the hall. 'Remember to dial 999, James!' she called after him.

She advanced into the room slowly, peering through the smoke, but couldn't see a thing. 'Dave!' she called. 'Are you there?'

There was no reply. She tried to feel for the sofa, but gave up because she was disoriented and kept barging into pieces of furniture which were seemingly in the wrong place. Just as she had felt her way back into the hall, a tongue of flame licked out of the room past her, and ran along the curtain shielding their clothes, turning it into a wall of fire.

I must get out of the flat, she thought, and turned to see Dave leaning against the lintel of the door. His hair was on fire, his face blackened. 'Oh, Dave!' she cried, and ran towards him, batting out the flames with her hands. She felt an immediate stinging pain in them, and tucked them into her armpits. Behind her she felt the heat from the burning clothes. 'Come on!' she said. 'We've got to get out!' He was coughing, and his eyes looked white against his blackened face. She took his hand and they stumbled along the hall, not speaking. James had shut the door, realizing that it would contain the fire. He was the only person with any sense, she thought, and it took her a few minutes to open it because of the pain in her hands.

'Come on, Dave!' she said. He was speechless, and she dragged him out with her and stumbled up the stairs, still holding his hand. The others were at the top.

'Good for you!' James came towards them. 'The fire brigade's on its way.' And then to Dave, 'You all right?'

Dave stared at him, not speaking, although his lips moved.

'He was there all the time!' Laurel said. They both looked at Dave, but he was holding himself stiffly, as if in shock.

Pat was still crying and clinging to James, but Jan and Damien came forward and helped Laurel to sit down on the wall with Dave. She felt like toppling off it, but steadied herself on the railings. There were other people there, and one held out a cup of tea and said, 'Drink that, it'll do you good.' She looked at Dave. He seemed to be in some sort of coma, his eyes staring straight ahead, and at that moment the fire engine came into the square. Suddenly there were lots of people there, being pushed back by the firemen, and then someone else was helping Dave and her into an ambulance, which had also appeared, its siren ringing eerily. The others were also shepherded in. They were all coughing.

'We'll probably be discharged,' Damien said, as if the situation was not new to him, 'but we'll have to be checked out first.' Laurel remembered he had gatecrashed.

She looked at Dave. His eyes were still white in his blackened face. His hair was burned, leaving bald patches, and he was shaking pitifully. Someone had put a blanket round him.

'You were brave getting him out,' Jan said.

'Yes, so you were,' Damien chimed in.

She tried to smile, then felt the tears running down her face, not for herself but for Dave, unable to face this scenario they were all involved in.

'Soon be at the hospital,' the man in uniform with them said. 'You've all been lucky, except...' He nodded towards Dave.

'We'd been having a party,' Pat said. She looked like a minstrel, with her face streaked with her tears, and her curls all awry.

'Dangerous things, parties,' the man said, looking at Dave again.

★ ★ ★

Laurel's father and mother came to visit her in hospital, her mother managing to look sympathetic and reproving at the same time. 'What a terrible thing to happen,' she said. 'We've visited Jan, she's living in Streatham with a friend, and she says to tell you that Dave Simpson is still in hospital.' She felt her face crumble.

Father said, 'We'll take you to see him, she gave us the address, and then you're coming back with us to recuperate. It must have been a terrible shock, the whole thing.' She nodded meekly.

'Are you ready to go?' Mother said.

'Yes,' she said. 'The nurse from the burns unit said I've to go to the one in Carlisle when I get home. I wondered where Dave had been moved to.'

'We'll drive you to see him first,' Father said.

Mother helped her to dress, careful with the hands, and put her arm round her when they were going down in the lift. She's really sorry for me, Laurel thought, but can't say it. So she said brightly, to cheer her up,

'Well, it could have been worse!'

The following day, they took her to see Dave. He was lying quite still and straight, his face and head covered with bandages. His eyes moved about like a mouse's behind them.

'Hello, chick,' he said. 'How do I look?'

'Fine,' she said. 'I'm so sorry, Dave,' she said. 'Is it bad?'

'Could be worse. It's my head. Can't seem to get it straight, hardly remember a thing. But Jan and Pat came to see me. They said you had tried to get me out.'

'But you got out yourself. My hands are better.' She held them up to show their new tender red skin. 'Yours will get like that. Don't worry. How are yours?'

'Not so good. Don't know if I'll be playing guitar again. If I can't, there's no point in living.' She saw his eyes fill with tears.

'They'll get better. Mine did. Keep cheerful. I shan't be able to come and see you again. They're taking me back with them.'

'Don't bother about that. I shan't be able to write, far less play. You go ahead and live your life.'

'Is that you brushing me off?'

'It's best. We're not suited. You've got family.' He closed his eyes and she sat still, waiting for him to open them again. He didn't, and after a time she got up from her chair and left.

1976

When Jake came in with her tea, he looked at her and said, 'You've been crying again.'

'It keeps coming back. His hopelessness, and me walking away and leaving him. And him dying...'

'Yes, that was tough.' He laid the tray down on a table and got in beside her, taking her in his arms. 'But look on the bright side. You came to Hong Kong to visit your brother, and then we met.'

Jake has everything, she thought, Dave had nothing, and I turned my back on him.

'And you spoke to me because of the thrushes,' she said.

'You looked so sad when that man walked past with the basket full of them.'

'And some of their heads and necks dangling through the holes. Poor thrushes. Poor Dave!' She remembered the scene clearly, sitting watching the boat people busy in their shops on the water, and the young man who sat down beside her turning to her and saying, 'Would you like to come to dinner with me if I promise not to offer you roast thrush?' And he held out a handkerchief.

She had laughed, and wiped her eyes, handing it back. She hoped he thought she was weeping for the thrushes. This crying bothered her a lot. Lability, Dr Barclay had called it.

'Well, I'm staying with my brother,' she said. 'They'll have dinner ready for me.'

'Is he married?'

'No, he has a partner, Chris. He's a great cook.'

'I see. Where do they live?'

'In an apartment opposite a park. I forget the name of it. But you can watch old men there doing tai chi,' she had said. 'Were you surprised at Nick's set-up?' she asked Jake now. She had taken him back to Nick's apartment in the end and he and Chris had

51

asked him to join them for dinner.

'Him being gay? Not at all. Some of my best friends are gay.'

'Did you notice how awkward my mother was about it when you came back to England with me?'

'It's the same in the backwoods of America.'

She laughed at him. 'If the people at home could hear you!'

He laughed with her. 'I read your mother's letter,' he said.

'Were you surprised at her saying she would like to come here?'

'Not at all. You've got a chip on your shoulder about your mother. It's not grown-up. And I didn't get the impression that she was running away, as you did.'

'She's never gone on holiday alone.'

'Perhaps it's for the best. It's my father's second marriage, as you know. Children and a husband got in the way of the magazine my mother runs. So they agreed to part amicably.'

'She's lovely. She spoke to me at our wedding.'

'Yes, Lia is elegant. My sisters see her in the city quite a lot, and she and I meet for lunch quite frequently. She's going to drop by, but says she doesn't want to intrude on love's young dream.'

'She's different from my mother. Not so anxious.'

'I liked her. She got on with Lia very well. I saw them talking together. Your father's an honest Joe, homely. We talked about climbing a lot. I think he's been very good at it, I shouldn't mind having a bash at those hills of yours.'

'Those hills are mountains, I'll have you know. He and Nick climbed together a lot. It runs in the family. My grandfather was well known for his prowess. I think that's why he started the shop for climbing gear. So you won't mind if Mother visits us?'

'Not at all. She could meet up with Joanne and Lia here, and use it as a base.'

'Well, I'll write and tell her. Maybe she'll have changed her mind by the time she gets my letter.'

'Not your mother, I should think. That's a lady who knows her own mind.'

Three

Sam opened Mary's gate and walked along the flagged path. There was no doubt about it, it was a much more appealing house than theirs. It was one of the original houses of the village, whitewashed, with black-painted window sills and frames. With its large garden, it seemed to sit comfortably in the valley, with the Borrowdale fells rising up, back and front, as if the house were in a comfortable nest. Bob Cass had been good at alterations, and had supervised the addition of a room opening off the kitchen, a huge garden room with magnificient views of the fells.

Looking at them today, blue-grey in the morning mist, Sam remembered many walks with Nick, one on their way to Great Gable when the rain had come down suddenly, and with it the mist, and Nick had panicked. He had sat him down on a stone, and seeing he was shaking and losing colour, had wrapped him in a foil cape from the first aid kit, and given him some hot tea from the flask. His grandfather, James, had been known locally as a fell climber, and perhaps with this in mind, he had been full of apologies. 'Please don't tell anyone, Dad,' he had said. He must have been only nine.

Most people who visited Mary never got past the garden room, he thought, having opened the door and gone in. It was comfortably furnished with chairs, sofas and tables laden with magazines, and plants everywhere. It had a general air of homeliness, so different from their own impeccable lounge, where the alteration of the angle of a chair or a cushion was all-important to Beth. He collapsed on the sofa, thinking he must water her orchids. 'Are you there, Mary?' he shouted.

Her voice came from the kitchen. 'The wanderer returns! I'll make some coffee and bring it out.'

'OK. I just feel like coffee this morning.'

In a few minutes she appeared carrying a tray, a medium-tall woman with a full bosom and untidy, fair curly hair which had escaped the band she had used to pull it back. She was smiling. 'Nice to see you. And you're brown. The weather was good?'

'Scorching.' He jumped up and placed a table in front of the sofa for the tray. 'Lovely to see you, Mary. We bathed a lot, and tried to keep out of the sun by touring. I hired a car, and we drove to Las Palmas, and to the other end of the island, and generally kept ourselves busy.'

'Did Beth like it?' She sat down beside him on the sofa.

'It gave her time to think. When we got back she said she had come to the conclusion that she wanted to get away from me.'

'Get away from you? Does she mean a divorce?'

'She didn't mention that word, nor did I. She's grown tired of the status quo, as she calls it.'

'Marriage?'

'Marriage for retired people. It doesn't come up to her expectations.'

'She doesn't know when she's well off. Bob died a week after he retired, so I never knew what it would have been like.'

'Yes, that was a shock. Mary,' he took her hands, 'I told her about that night.'

'Oh, why did you do that? Was that what sparked it off?'

'No, she had made up her mind before that, but it makes it easier for her. She can blame me now. The unfaithful husband.'

'We agreed at the time that we would never tell anyone, let alone Beth.'

'I know, but it just came out...How do you feel about me?'

'You know how I feel, after that. But as I said then, I would never break up anyone's marriage.'

'If Beth goes away, would you come and live with me in my house?'

'No, I couldn't do that.' She shook her head. 'Besides, I would feel like a usurper. And I don't like your house. It's too grand. All that facing of stone on brick. It's not right in the Lakes.'

'Blame my father. He saw himself as a success in Wetherham, and felt he had to have an imposing house.'

'They were off-comers. They brought their ideas about building with them from the south. Had he never heard of slate?'

'Only for roofs. I rather think it was my mother who was responsible. He had fallen in love with the Lakes when he came climbing, and decided to start a sports out-fitters in Wetherham. He had always been a great climber abroad, and then when he came here he got hold of Wainwright's books, and was hooked.'

'The interior is Beth's. I'm only comfort-able in my own house. No.' She shook her head. 'It wouldn't suit me. Beth would have a foot in both camps. She could arrive at any time.' She paused. 'You could come here if you like.'

'Wouldn't you worry about people talk-ing?' he asked.

'I would have to think about that.'

'Perhaps we could be discreet.'

'Is that possible in this village?' She met

his eyes. Hers were steadily grey, and he had always liked her eyes with their dark lashes, which he suspected she dyed since her hair was naturally fair. She paused. 'But that means you would both be keeping a foot in either camp. If she wants to leave a door open so that she can return to you, and you came here, ready to run back, where does that leave me?'

'I see that.' He looked at her, and thought how pink her mouth was against the fair skin. A woman to sleep with, comforting, comfortable.

'And you have two children. You would have to tell them.'

'Not necessarily. Would you marry me if Beth and I got a divorce?'

'Now, that's a question I'd need notice of. I've got Rachel and William. I would have to tell them. Although they're both married, they like to think of coming here with the children, because they were children here themselves.'

'I can see the ball's in our court – I mean, Beth and me. Am I willing to let her go and swan about and come back and expect to find me where she left me, or should we split up properly? Is that it?'

'That's it. She'll go off, will Beth, if she says she will, I know, but you would have to say that she needn't expect to find you there when she comes back.'

Sam looked at her. He had never thought of Mary being at all like Beth, but here she was, pointing things out to him which he ought to have realized.

'If I were divorced, would you marry me, Mary?'

She looked dubious, he thought. 'I'd have to think it out, Sam, and possibly talk to the children.'

'Yours are handy. Both of ours are far away so we can't do that. Although I think Beth intends to visit them.' He looked at his watch. Lunch time.

'What you have to decide, Sam, is do you want to marry me? It becomes more a matter of pros and cons when we're both in our fifties. One gets sense then.'

'Yes, I feel I've come to you with a situation which I haven't thought through.' He took her by the shoulders and kissed her. 'How does that feel to you?'

'Fine. But don't forget I'm not often kissed by a man now. You're at it all the time.'

'Not really. It's been a case of all passion spent for a long time with Beth. I think it was because of you.'

'That you'll have to be sure about.'

He got up and looked down at her. 'At the moment, I love you.'

'To the exclusion of Beth?'

He couldn't answer that. 'You would have to put yourself to the test too. How much did you miss Bob when he died?'

'Well, I slept with you, didn't I? I was feeling...deprived. I didn't think at times I could weather it, but I did, and I'm quite proud of myself, except for that one slip.'

'But you enjoyed being with me?'

'Sleeping with you? Yes, that was fine. But I shouldn't like to marry you for that reason. Indeed, I'd be reluctant to give up the independence I've made for myself. If I were you, I should try it out while Beth is away before you start filling her place.'

He looked at her. 'I can see why people say

you're good on committees.'

She laughed. 'You learn to rely on your own judgement when you're alone, and then you become good at it for others.'

Four

Beth was busy packing in her bedroom. Sam was in his shed, doing what he always did there in summer – pottering. The loft extension was for winter. Laurel had begged her to go ahead with it, but, what a mess! Never again. She had been right that the upheaval would be terrible – and the dust. But, certainly, it did get rid of his papers in the lounge. And no doubt it had increased the value of the property.

Now that it had reached this stage, she reflected that novels and so on never told you how people parted – the practical side of it. Perhaps because it was too painful, she thought. The little details: this packing she was doing, counting her knickers, the decision as to which dresses and trousers to take, then the photographs, ending by denuding the bedroom, and then feeling that that's not fair to Sam and leaving one of her with Laurel and Nicholas the day he went off to university. She saw she was wearing her first trouser suit. She had always been able to wear trousers, fortunately, unlike Mary Cass, who preferred skirts. 'From the waist down,' she'd said, 'I'm hopeless. Hips, calves, they're all better disguised with a skirt.' Ah, well, he should be comfortable with Mary. No leanness there. A big bosom. A change for Sam.

But he had said that Mary didn't want a situation like this, with him popping in and out. Her going away left all of them in a doubtful situation, but she didn't see that. Hadn't she gone away to Kent for weeks when her mother had been ill, and no one had queried that? But that situation had been entirely different, she chided herself.

An extended visit to Laurel and Nicholas was surely a good enough excuse. But to leave one's husband behind? He could say to friends that it was both of their choice, and after all, was it anyone's business?

She had been in Kent for six weeks when

her mother was dying of cancer. Perhaps she was the only one who had had doubts, not about leaving Sam, but about leaving Kent to marry him in the first place. 'The garden of England' had never seemed more appropriate when compared with the roughness and the rain in Borrowdale. And her friends in Maidstone had all seemed so sophisticated, and even sorry for her, implying that she was buried 'up North' as they called it, with the Herdwick sheep, far away from airports and Channel crossings, which were so convenient 'down South'.

She looked round the room. There was nothing else, so she clicked and shut the locks of her cases, and sat down on the bed to check her passport, tickets, travellers' cheques and money. Handkerchief for the look of the thing. Tissues in one of the cases, she remembered.

She concentrated on applying her mind to the items in her case, really concentrated, then heaved a sigh. Yes, everything was there. Presents. The only thing she hadn't packed was an umbrella, but she could surely borrow one. Hong Kong would be hot and rainless, she expected. She wasn't so sure about New York. Both Nicholas and Laurel had said they would be delighted to see her, but had Nicholas's letter been as explicit as Laurel's, who had talked about plans she would make for her, people to visit? Nicholas had said nothing like that, just: 'You'll like Hong Kong. I can show you the sights.'

She went downstairs and through the kitchen to the back door for the last time, she thought – but not for an ordinary holiday, she reminded herself. A trial separation, she would call it in her mind. What was Sam calling it, now that he had revealed to her his relationship with Mary?

She went down the garden path and pushed open the door of the shed. It was always stuck, and Sam, looking up, put down what he was holding and came quickly. He wrenched it open and looked at her.

'Should see to that,' he said. His expression was faintly bashful but smiling, like the young Sam who had courted her long ago. He's flummoxed by the situation I've created, she thought, he doesn't know if I'm deserting him for good, or for an extended holiday.

'I'm ready, Sam,' she said. 'Would you carry my cases down and put them in the car?' Then, when in the kitchen, she said, 'Perhaps we should have a coffee before we leave. It's a long drive to Manchester.'

He shook his head. 'We'll have plenty of time there before you get on the plane. I'm not quite sure how long it will take me. It varies, depending on the traffic on the motorways.'

'I know. Well, in that case, I'm ready. If you go upstairs and get the cases, I'll pay a last visit to the loo.' She laughed, feeling embarrassed, and left the kitchen.

When she came back he had stowed everything away in the car, and was standing behind the front door. She went towards him. 'Well, this is it, Sam,' she said. *What are you doing?* The words echoed in her brain.

'I can't believe this,' he said. 'You wouldn't like to change your mind?'

'No, not now that I've got this far.' She had an immense desire to throw her arms round his neck and say, 'Ask me to stay', but knew by his set face that it was too late.

What am I doing? The words wouldn't go away, and to drown them she said, 'Well, let's go.' He opened the door for her and she preceded him down the drive to the car.

Mrs Cochrane, true to type, was standing at her open door. She would have been hiding behind the curtains for the last hour, in case she missed Beth's departure. 'Have a nice holiday, Beth.' She came forward. 'I'll miss you popping in.' Her old face crumpled.

'Thanks, Mrs Cochrane. I'll send you cards.' It had always been 'Mrs'. 'Sam will keep an eye on you, don't worry.'

'Yes, I'll be calling tomorrow. I haven't forgotten Tuesday's our shopping day,' Sam shouted. He always remembered she was deaf.

'Well, goodbye, Beth.' Mrs Cochrane was now at the fence dividing their gardens. 'I have a little present for you.' She handed over a plastic tube, which Beth could see contained rolled-up handkerchiefs.

'How thoughtful of you. Do you know,

I've forgotten to pack any. I'll pop this in my handbag. Thank you very much.' She extended her hand over the fence and grasped the old, dry one of Mrs Cochrane's. 'You take care of yourself. Goodbye. Be good.' Which was a ridiculous thing to say to an eighty-year-old.

'Goodbye. And don't worry about that husband of yours. I'll keep an eye on him for you.'

'That's kind. Goodbye. Keep well.'

'Don't forget to come back.' Was that a knowing look in the old eyes?

Sam had inherited the business and the house when his parents had 'passed on', as they said in these parts, and it often seemed to Beth that she had inherited Mrs Cochrane as well. She had been a close friend of Mrs Crome, her mother-in-law, who had asked Beth to keep an eye on her, should she go. She did her best, but Mrs Cochrane's inquisitiveness was hard to bear.

Driving through the village, she badly wanted to cry. It was so familiar, the hotel where the fell races started from, the post office-cum-general store, the bus stop with its shelter and, as usual, a few drenched walkers sheltering. When Sam slowed down to cross the bridge, she saw Mrs Cairns and Mrs Lyle, friends of Mrs Cochrane's, standing together, gossiping. Mrs Cairns looked round in time to see the car passing, and Beth said to Sam, 'We've been spotted. She'll be able to make something out of that. You rarely drive me.'

One side of Sam's face went up. 'Miss Marple,' he said.

And there was the village hall, a wooden structure which Sam's father had given to the village, and where Laurel had been such a success as little Red Riding Hood when she was six.

And now they were driving along the road to Wetherham. The town was only six miles away, which had suited Sam for the shop. Goodbye mountains, she said to herself. She had to admit that no place she ever visited gave her quite such a feeling of space – she remembered how she had had a feeling of claustrophobia when she first came to live here from Kent, but now on the rare occasions when she went to London she felt stifled. The air there smelled of too many bodies and petrol fumes. It had taken all of five years to get used to living 'up north'.

The circular route round the town which they were now on deprived her of a last look at the shop. And the town centre which she liked, with its wide pavements and general air of country bustle. However, one couldn't compare the Moot Hall with Leeds Castle, she thought, for grandeur.

She had always enjoyed going to the shop, and seeing all the climbing gear on sale. The profits depended on the devotees of the Lake District, the walkers and the climbers, and they had to be provided for. Miss Baxter, the buyer, had generally laid aside something for Nicholas and Laurel when they had been children – anoraks and climbing gear – and she had always looked out for shoes for Beth, knowing her taste, nothing too heavy – stylish walking shoes. She felt nostalgic, remembering. Should she have called in to say goodbye to Miss Baxter who had become a friend, at least she was invited to the parties they gave? But no, that would have made too much of her going away.

The road which she knew so well slipped past. It was amazing the miles she drove to visit friends all over Lakeland; it was necessary. People who said, 'It must be quiet in the Lakes', didn't know what they were talking about. You had to search for culture – a piano recital, a play, an exhibition. A life went on under the constant crowds of visitors, almost all year now. One kept indoors during weekends, or invited friends. It was one's home environment, a background, one adapted to it, and only missed the feeling of space if one went away. She was surprised to find herself thinking like that, like a native, remembering how difficult it had been to adapt when she married Sam, and how she had been regarded as an incomer in the village.

She caught a last glimpse of Derwent Water with the sky reflected in it and thought, admit it Beth, you've grown to love it here. You would have to include that if you decided to leave Sam. They were driving past the Lodore Falls Hotel where they'd had a party for their retirement, and remembering the congratulations they'd received reminded her how happy she had been that night. *What are you doing, Beth Crome?* she asked herself.

Now they were running along by Thirlmere, which she never thought of as a real 'Lakes' lake as it was man-made; now there was the feeling of leaving grandeur behind her and dropping into Grasmere, into tourist country, Wordsworth country, Ambleside and Windermere; now they had really descended and were making for Kendal, skirting it, and on to the motorway. Sam increased his speed. He was a fast, sure driver; he always gave her a feeling of confidence. *Tell him you're feeling sad, that you're going to miss all this, and him...*

This is a situation I recognize, she thought. We're alone together in the car, and I haven't anything to say, even on a momentous occasion like this. Keep quiet and see if he speaks first. The time passed. They rolled up the miles. Lancaster now, soon be Preston, then Manchester. *No, I'll wait until he breaks the silence.*

'How do you feel?' Sam said.

73

'Miserable.' And surprising herself, because it wasn't what she had been thinking at all, 'I was thinking of when Rosemary and I stayed near your village – at your suggestion, I may say. We had met at the shop, remember, and you asked us to come to a dance being held for the fell races. You were a steward...'

'And I had no eyes for anyone but you, and I got Ron Seville to join us, so that I could have you to myself...'

'They didn't hit it off.'

'No, but we did. Dancing in that tent with the Lakeland Boys playing, or whatever they were called, made me think I was in heaven...'

'Heaven, heaven...' she sang. 'That was a Fred Astaire song.'

'I certainly didn't dance like him. And there was a huge moon when I walked you back to your hotel, and we could hear the rippling beck when we sat on the wall, remember?'

'And those huge crags, or fells, or whatever you call them, menacing me...'

'But you like them now?'

'Yes, they've become friends, although I could never bring myself to join you in those fell walks you did. The mist scared me when you took me for the first time. The mist and the menacing stillness...'

'There's nothing like it. But it isn't menacing, you get a high every time you go up.'

'Too high for me.'

They stopped talking, and the misery came back. Why was she doing this? Because she had made up her mind in Gran Canaria, and foolishly talked about it to Sam. But how do you *really* feel, Beth, she asked herself. Have you changed your mind about your marriage to him or not? Are you regretting this already? You still have time to turn back. You're not on the plane yet.

'Should be there in ten minutes,' Sam said. 'Two hours to spare.'

'Good,' she said, thinking she still had time...Well, they had talked a little, which was something.

Five

Beth settled herself down in her seat on the plane. I'm becoming quite good at this, she thought. The last time she had flown to New York was with Sam for Laurel's wedding, and before that to visit the Stansbys at Long Island. She had a window seat, and the man on her left was late middle-aged. I hope he doesn't start talking, she thought. He was busy, like her, settling in, getting papers from his case, rising to put the case in the locker, sitting down again. She folded her jacket on her lap. That wasn't going to do. She should have asked the stewardess to put it in the locker for her.

'Would you like me to put that in the locker for you?' Her fellow passenger was pointing at the jacket, as if he guessed what she was thinking.

'Would you? That's kind.' She handed over the jacket, a white three-quarter one, which she had worn at the last minute thinking it would be suitable for New York.

'No trouble.' He got up again, she heard the click as he opened the locker, and then he sat down. 'You have to be comfortable when travelling.'

'That's true.'

'Do you fly often?'

'No, but recently yes. I visited friends in Long Island, then back again to New York, and after that to Gran Canaria.'

'So you know New York?'

'I'm familiar with it. I'll get to know it better this time. My daughter's apartment is on the East Side.'

'Near the park?'

'Quite near, I think.' That's enough about me. Should I ask questions now? she wondered. Her intentions were interrupted by a stewardess taking up her position in front of the bulkhead and beginning a demonstration of the safety precautions. Beth watched intently, but the man beside her was going through his papers once again, and didn't seem to be paying much attention.

She didn't want to speak after that, since they were taking off, and she sat straight while the captain was giving directions to the crew ready for take-off. Sam had put his hand over hers the last few times, knowing that she was nervous.

Once in the air she relaxed and said, 'Well, that's us airborne.' The remark sounded superfluous, as if she was pretending to be *au fait* with the proceedings. She smiled at the man.

'You don't like flying?' he said.

'I suppose I haven't much experience, but now that my children are abroad, I expect I'll be flying fairly often.'

'Live for the moment, and don't let your mind wander on possibilities, that's the best way. How about a relaxing drink?' The trolley manned by two stewards had appeared at their seats.

'I'd like that. White wine, dry, please,' she said, and rummaged in her bag for some money.

'This one's on the house,' he said. And to the steward, 'Same for me, please.' She felt a fool as she watched the steward pouring the drinks.

'Thank you very much,' Beth said as the man placed the drink in front of her.

'Do *you* fly often?' She didn't want to divulge any more information about herself. She had already revealed herself as a tyro.

'Once a month. I have an export business.'

'It'll be like taking a bus to you.'

'My wife doesn't like me being away.'

'Why is that?' she asked. Let's see what he says to that, she thought.

'She wants me to retire, give up the business and hand it over to my son.'

'Does your son want that?'

'I think he'd like the travelling, but as it happens he's just got himself married, and I think *his* wife would object.'

'These women!' Beth said, smiling.

'Where would we be without them?' He raised his glass to her, giving her an appreciative glance, and she thought, this is why he likes travelling – chance encounters, and the freedom it gives him.

'My husband and I retired recently.'

'You both wanted to?'

'Yes, my husband likes it. I think more than me.' Goodness, she thought, is that a come on? 'Men who like the thought of retirement have generally been planning for it, they have all kinds of tasks piled up in their minds, whereas women – especially if they have been working, as I was – have managed to juggle those tasks at home along with their working life.'

'My wife didn't work, so she's looking forward to my company.'

'Yes, I can see that. Women aren't much good at travelling alone, or should I say, married women.'

'And yet you're doing it?' He smiled at her.

'It's only to visit my children – my daughter in New York and then my son in Hong Kong.'

'Hong Kong?' he said appreciatively, his eyes lighting up. 'And your husband didn't want to accompany you?'

This was a facer, the sort of thing friends at home would be puzzling over. What should she say? 'He wasn't asked.' 'He didn't offer to come.' No, neither of these were any good. She compromised. 'Actually, we'd been on two trips quite close to each other, and he's really a stay-at-home person.'

'But you're not?'

She would have to switch the conversation to him, she thought, but luckily the two stewards appeared again with the food trolley this time, and there was the general bustle of arranging the shelves to support their trays, and being asked about their choice of food and drinks.

'This is the bit where you get a surprise,' the man said as the stewardess handed over their trays and then drinks. 'It never looks like what you chose. Camouflage. By the way,' he held out his hand, 'I'm Reggie Connor.'

She took it. 'Beth Crome.'

'Now we know each other much better,' he said. He looked so much at ease as he tackled his meal that Beth thought, he's used to this, meeting people on planes, whereas I'm not. That's because you're defensive, she told herself. She remembered a saying she had heard Laurel use – go with the flow.

They were silent while they ate, but the wine relaxed her and she thought, if you're going to be on your own this is good practice for you. She should make the most of encounters like this. She always complained that Sam didn't talk. And then he'd said that she despised him...She didn't like to think of that.

'Have you any more family?' she asked this Reggie Connor. 'You mentioned a son.'

'No, unfortunately. I should have liked a daughter.'

'I've got one of each,' she said.

'And you said your son was in Hong Kong?'

'Yes, I've never been there.'

'Oh, you'll like it. It's so bustling and cosmopolitan.'

'Yes, I gather that from Nicholas. He flies all over from there. His firm, a travel company, is based there.'

'That sounds like an interesting job. Is he married?'

'No.' She knew she was defensive about Nicholas.

'He'll be lucky if he escapes it there. The Hong Kong girls are, well, captivating.' His eyes lit up.

'I don't think that would suit Nicholas.' She worried that she had implied that Nicholas was gay.

Suddenly she didn't like Reggie Connor, nor the fact that she was stuck with him for an unconscionable time. She realized that she was missing Sam. He had been such a good buffer.

'How did you like the food?' Reggie Connor asked.

'I happen to like chicken. It's not organic, but they've done their best with it.' She thought of James, the farmer near them, who obligingly killed a fowl and dressed it for them when asked.

'If you wash it down with wine it's all right.' Mr Connor refilled her glass. He launched into a description of the restaurants in New York that were worth going to. She tried to look interested, but felt a headache developing. If Sam had been on her other side...But there weren't three seats together, as there had been on their flight to

Gran Canaria, when Sam had kept a talkative woman happy by listening intently. He had sat between her and Beth. I'm beginning to see the difficulties of a single woman travelling alone, she thought. At least someone of her age. When she had been young, it hadn't been like that. Every meeting had been an adventure, but then if she had been young, she wouldn't have carried on a conversation with a man like Reggie Connor. She felt exposed without Sam, she had to admit to herself. I'm missing marital solidarity.

Rosemary Conway. The name popped into her memory. That's what had been puzzling her. The same initials as this man. She and Beth had been on a walking tour in the Lakes. Rosemary Conway, fat, fair, a contrast to slim, dark Beth, they had had different reasons for going on a walking tour. Rosemary's had been for exercise, Beth's had been curiosity, because she had never been out of the south. There had been a romantic appeal, possibly because of her reading.

They had gone into Sam's shop to buy sun

cream, Beth arguing that a shop like this would know what walkers used. While they had been talking to the assistant, Sam had appeared at his side. 'I know just what you want,' he had said, producing a tube. 'This is the best one for your purpose.'

She had liked him, his bright eyes, his tanned face. They had chatted for a time and he had advised them on walks in the district. 'He certainly had his eyes on you,' Rosemary had said.

A few days later, when Beth was in the bank alone, Rosemary having said she was going to soak in a bath to get rid of her aches and pains, she had met Sam again. He had recognized her and said, 'What luck meeting you! How did you get on with your walk?' They had talked, delighting in each other, and she had gone back to the hotel, walking on air. She had never met anyone like him before; he made the young men she had known before seem weedy city types.

She said to Rosemary on her return, 'I met the man in the sports shop, the one who recommended the sun cream, and guess what, he's asked me out!'

'Your eyes are shining,' Rosemary had said. 'It must be love.' It had been. A swift courtship, with hesitation on her part because the Lakes had seemed to her so remote from the background she knew. But her love had been genuine enough and urgent enough to give in. She had never met anyone like Sam before; he had all the rugged qualities you would expect from his background. He was like a breath of fresh air, she told herself, and she was easily persuaded into marriage. Sam had been conventional, more so than her, and wanted her legally, as he often said. She wanted him.

To adopt that background for herself took a little more persuasion, and to live so far from London was difficult to imagine, but her love for him won her over. She simply couldn't live without him, she decided. In the end, the landscape and Sam had won.

When their trays had been taken away, she got up, excusing herself to Reggie Connor, and went to the toilet. Putting powder on her face, she worked out her strategy. She would be polite but distant, as befitted her age. That was the trouble about growing older, you felt you were often playing a younger role and making yourself look ridiculous. When she squeezed into her seat again she said to Reggie Connor, who had looked up with a welcoming smile, 'I'm rather tired. I was up early to catch the plane. I think I'll have a snooze.'

'You do that,' he said, and took a magazine from the back pocket of the seat in front.

To her surprise, after examining her behaviour for a few moments and thinking of Sam, that remark of his popped up again. 'You despise me,' he had said. Why did it hurt so much? Had it been because she had often implied that they were backward up in the north, and she knew some of their woman friends made remarks about her attitudes, the general implication being that she was snobbish? Or was it because she and Sam had been together so long that they had begun to think of each other as individuals, not as part of a couple? But wasn't he right in his remark? No, she thought, I never despised him, though I may have been critical. But she admitted now that he was entitled to be what he was, without criticism from her. Give him his due, she thought now, he never criticized her.

But he had found solace with Mary Cass, which in a way was a kind of criticism. She knew Mary was easy-going, not critical, generally liked, whereas Beth didn't know how she was regarded by other people. Were they afraid of her opinions, which she often stated with utter conviction, as she knew? Men didn't like women to express their opinions in the circles they moved in – shopkeepers, solicitors, doctors and the like – and she often felt that in mixed company she was doing just that, had seen women looking at her as if she was *daring*. The thing is, she thought, I'm not comfortable to be with, people are chary of me. I show my dislike of joining the women in their eternal talk of houses and children. It seemed that sitting here in space, she had time to see herself as she was and she had never done that at home.

Had Sam felt she relegated him to his own space? She remembered her mother telling her of a farmer's wife she knew who used to spread newspapers on the linoleum floor of her kitchen, telling her husband to take off his boots before he dare walk in. People had felt sorry for him. Henpecked, they called him. But that's surely an ancient story, she thought. She analysed the word 'henpecked', savouring its meaning, thinking, I don't get time to think like this at home. There was a question at the back of her mind. 'Why did you walk out on your husband?' Mary Cass wasn't the reason. She had made up her mind in Gran Canaria, before she knew about the liaison, as they called it.

She thought it was then, faced with an impasse, that she had gone to sleep, and when she woke and looked at her watch, she realized it was near the time of arrival. It took her a minute to reorient herself.

'Had a good nap?' Reggie Connor asked.

'I'm surprised at the time,' she said. 'We're nearly there! I must have been more tired with the early start than I realized.'

'Yes, we're not far off. I've enjoyed meeting you, Beth Crome. We seemed to get on well. Perhaps if you get lonely, you'd like to give me a call?' He fumbled in his inside pocket and produced a card. She looked at it. R. CONNOR & SON. EXPORTERS, 1 WALNUT GROVE, QUEENS, NY

'That's near New York,' she said.

'Yes, but I come in each day. I could give you lunch. Does your daughter work?'

'Yes, she does. Downtown, as she calls it.'

'You'll probably find that she and her husband clear off each morning and you'll be left wondering what to do with yourself.'

'Oh, I don't think so. She's got a programme ready for me.' She was aware of the plane swooping down, of holding her breath, releasing it. Then there was a bump; they had landed.

'Let me get your jacket,' Reggie Connor said, springing up. She saw he was broad in the beam as he stretched up to the locker, the vent in his jacket splitting. 'Is there someone meeting you?' he asked when he helped her into her jacket.

'Yes, my daughter.'

She said goodbye, and managed to fit herself into the queue making its way out. She had to follow people and do what they did – queue at the various counters, collect luggage at the carousel, go through the appropriate gates. On previous trips she had simply followed Sam, not using her head, and she was surprised that she hadn't bothered. Marital solidarity again, she thought.

To her surprise she found herself at last in a line at the exit, going through the barriers to where crowds of people stood – looking at them, she thought, as if they had arrived from outer space. She picked out Laurel at once by her fair hair – surely fairer than before, at least there were now golden streaks in it – and dressed in a stone-coloured suit which looked New-York smart. She was waving enthusiastically. When they met, they hugged, and Beth was surprised that tears flooded her eyes at the sight of this lovely daughter of hers so exquisitely dressed, and with the gold jewellery which looked genuine – so different from that bedraggled girl they had brought home from London after the fire.

'Everything went all right, Mum?' she was saying as she took her case. 'Come along, I've got the car parked outside. Jake gave it to me to pick you up. How's Dad?'

'Fine when I left him. How's Jake?'

'Fine when I left him.' She had always been one for a joke.

Six

'So that's St Patrick's Cathedral?' Beth said.
'I've heard about it. The traffic's terrible,
Laurel. How do you manage to drive in
New York?'

'Jake insisted on it. He says it's no worse
than any big city, forgetting that our nearest
is Carlisle! The only thing you've to worry
about is the one-way system and taxi-
drivers, he says. I drove him to San Francis-
co once, and then he said I was ready for
New York.'

'So he bosses you about?'

'No, he does not, Mother.' She had caught
the implied criticism in her voice, Beth
realized. I must be careful.

They parked in the underground car park
of the apartment block on 57th Street,
where Laurel and Jake lived, and took a lift

up to the foyer. It looked grand to Beth – marble floors, shrubs and even trees in containers, and commissionaires. One of them came towards them.

'Anything I can do, Mrs Stansby?'

'No thanks, Webster. This is my mother, Mrs Crome. She'll be going out and in quite a lot.'

'I'll look out for her.' And, taking Beth's cases and leading them towards the lift, he said to her, 'Just flew in, Mrs Crome?'

'Yes, from London.' She returned his smile.

The apartment was as she had visualized it. Large, sparsely furnished, no nick-nacks, – well, you only gathered these after a long marriage, she thought. Laurel showed her into her bedroom.

'There's a shower in there, Mum, if you want to freshen up,' she said, opening a door off the bedroom. 'Just make yourself at home.'

'OK.' They were a little shy of each other, but once Beth had unpacked her dressing gown and a black dress she liked, she went back into the lounge. 'Laurel?' she called.

'In the kitchen,' came her voice.

She found Laurel in a gleaming kitchen, busy with a food processor. She looked up. 'The dinner's all prepared, but I'm just whipping this up for a lemon meringue pie. One of your recipes. It's a favourite with Jake.'

'Good.' She looked around. 'This is nice. Can I help?'

'No, thanks.'

'Your flat's lovely.' She thought Laurel had looked enquiringly at her. 'When does Jake come in?'

'Any minute. I'm going to change into my running gear and get out of this.' She had taken off the jacket of her suit, and kicked aside her high-heeled pumps. 'We run for half an hour every evening along the East River. You won't mind?'

'No, not at all.'

'I'll finish this, and if you have your shower, we'll have a drink when Jake gets in. We're having Lia, his mother, for dinner, and my boss, Joe Galliano.'

'Your boss?'

'Yes, I met him at Long Island. He's a

95

friend of the family. He has a gallery down-town, and he needed someone for the front of house, so to speak – a receptionist – so he asked me. I'm learning a lot about art. We're near the Met here, and I slip in from time to time.'

'I'd love to go there.'

'We'll do that. Remember how you used to trail me around London when we went, usually to shop, but you always fitted in some galleries. Impressionists.'

'Yes, I was always keen on them.'

'Joe's stuff is modern, but if he got his hands on a Matisse, I'm sure he would sell his soul for it. Well, that's that.' She wiped her hands on a towel, looked at Beth. 'Dad all right when you left?'

'Yes, fine.'

'He didn't want to come with you?'

'No, you know Dad. A full diary, and he's not fond of leaving the house too much.' She felt Laurel's eyes on her.

'Yes. Give him a ring, if you like. There's a telephone in your bedroom. Shall we both go and tidy ourselves up? Jake will be here soon.'

'Right. I'll phone Dad, if I may.' She hadn't thought of doing that. Back in her room she dialled their home number, and in a second or two heard Sam's voice.

'Beth! You arrived safely?'

'Yes. Good trip. Laurel suggested I should give you a ring.'

'How is she?'

'Very different from the girl we brought back from London. Elegant, self-assured, and their flat is so modern, really what I expected.' There was a pause. 'I'll ring off, Sam. It was Laurel who suggested I ring you, but I don't know what calls cost from here, I'm phoning from my bedroom. Goodbye.' She felt terrible. It would have been better not to have called him at all, than to have hung up so precipitately. It had been Laurel's suggestion. Families! She had no intention of keeping in touch with Sam, reporting every move she made. Now he knew she was here, that was the end.

She heard voices and laughter. Jake must be home, she thought. She changed into the black dress and put on some diamanté earrings that Sam had given her on her last birthday. She brushed her hair, made up her face and looked at herself in the mirror. What would Jake think of her when he saw her? Would she look hopelessly provincial, old? And should she have had her hair completely bleached, instead of those blonde streaks to cover the grey? A very British cut, she thought, but it would have to do.

She sat down and sorted out the contents of her bag. She only needed a comb, one of Mrs Cochrane's handkerchiefs, lipstick, mirror and powder for this evening, and she searched in her case for a smaller black bag she had brought with her. The large one she tucked away in one of the sliding cupboards. One more look in the long mirror. If only Sam were here, she thought. He had always been good at entering rooms, went in smiling, head up, like a well loved dog, sure of his welcome.

She opened the door and went into the lounge. There was no one there. She sat down on the white leather sofa, her knees together, and waited.

She didn't have long to wait. In a few

minutes Jake and Laurel appeared from their room, both dressed in running gear. Laurel, she noticed, was wearing a scarlet cap with a pompom on top, more for appearance than anything else, Beth thought. Her hair hung round it like a schoolgirl's.

'Well, look at you!' Jake came towards her. 'How are you, Beth? Had a good trip?'

She got up and he gave her a bear hug. 'Fine, to both questions. You look very fit, Jake,' she said.

'So I should be. Laurel looks after me so well. Drags me out to run when I'm tired out.'

'Don't listen to him, Mum. He's a tease. Go and get the drinks, Jake.'

'Yes, of course, your mother needs one after that long journey. Did you meet anyone on the plane, Beth?'

'Actually, there was a man sitting beside me. He gave me his card. Lived in Queens, I think.'

'Never trust anyone who comes from Queens. I'm surprised Sam lets you loose. Wasn't he afraid?'

'Yes, Mum,' Laurel joined in, as if it had

been arranged. 'What did he think of you coming here on your own?'

'Don't answer that till you tell me what you want to drink, Beth,' Jake said.

'Does a gin and tonic sound terribly old-fashioned to a New Yorker?'

'Not at all. My stepmother, Joanne, likes that. Your usual white wine, darling?' he asked Laurel.

'Yes, please. Did you buy more for tonight? It's shellfish.'

'Yes, I didn't forget. Do you see how she bullies me, Beth?' What a charmer he was, she thought. She hoped he was good to Laurel. But they did seem devoted to each other. 'And before I went to the office this morning, it was, "Would you set the table, Jake?"'

'Don't expect sympathy from my mother,' Laurel said. 'She's all in favour of men doing their bit, aren't you, Mum?'

'I worked for a few years before I retired, Jake. I had taken time off when the children were small. Sam got very good at cooking. Remember his toad-in-the-hole, Laurel?'

'Yes, and his treacle tart, yum-yum!'

'I'm obviously very ill educated,' Jake said. 'My mother was always too busy, so we had a cook.' There was the sound of a buzzer in the room, and Jake walked across to the intercom. Beth heard him say, 'Mother! Come on up.' In a few minutes she was in the room. 'You remember Lia, don't you, Beth?' Jake said, leading her forward.

'Of course I do.' She had been impressed by Lia Harvey – tall, dark-haired, elegant. When they had met at the wedding her hair had been up, showing off the fine planes of her face and the large, dark eyes. Today her hair was loose, making her look younger, and her smile was engaging.

'How are you, Beth?' she said. 'Nice to meet you again.'

'Very well, thank you.' They kissed.

'Isn't this lovely?' Lia Harvey looked round, smiling, then turned back to Beth. 'So you've left that charming man of yours behind?'

'I was just asking her about Dad,' Laurel said. She leant forward towards Beth, seated on the sofa, reminding her of the younger Laurel when she had wanted to know something. 'Did you ask him to come, Mum?' she said.

'It wasn't necessary.' She looked to Lia for support.

'You haven't been married long enough to understand, Laurel. When you've been married for a long time, you long to taste independence again.'

'I...just made up my mind to come alone,' Beth said.

'Did Dad not mind?' Tiresome girl.

'You know Dad, he's always a project ahead.' Now it's Mary, Beth thought.

Jake broke in. 'I've got your vodka ready, Mother.' He went to the tray and brought her a glass. 'Here's a lady,' he gestured at Lia, 'who just took off from my father, without asking Nancy, Claire, or me.'

'Yes.' She had a throaty laugh. 'I was naughty. But I didn't desert you. I saw that you were well cared for.'

'Joe's coming,' Laurel said, changing the subject. 'We'll leave you two to entertain him until we get back.'

'Are you running in the park?' Lia asked.

'No, East River,' Jake said.

'But we shan't be long,' Laurel said. 'It's your son who feels he needs it after a hard day at the office.'

'Off you go, then. Beth and I will have a nice tête-à-tête while you're away.'

'There's bourbon there for when Joe comes,' Jake said. 'Come along, Laurel.'

'I'm ready.' She got up. 'Enjoy yourselves,' she said to the two women.

When they had gone, Lia said, 'She's a lovely girl, Beth. I'm so glad for Jake. He's chosen well. Luckily he needs pushing around.'

Was she implying that Laurel was bossy? Beth wondered. 'Yes,' she said, 'Laurel has always known her own mind.'

'I met your son at the wedding. He's in Hong Kong?'

'Yes. I'm going to see Nicholas as well. I want to have a talk with both children.'

Lia looked at her over her glass. 'Take my advice, don't ask your children for their opinion. It's what suits you that's important.'

'I think you're seeing through me.' Beth smiled.

'No, I don't flatter myself. But I left Bob, as you know, by mutual consent, and I didn't consult my children about it. It's been a complete success, for them as well. We live in a different world now. They have their own life. It's hard for our age group to realize that. Is there a man involved?'

Beth smiled. 'No, no man. I'll tell you why I'm here, and then you'll understand. No, there isn't another man involved. I was on holiday with Sam and it suddenly struck me that I had a lot of life ahead, but the idea of living that with Sam suddenly didn't appeal to me, so I decided to take time off to think about it.'

'That was risky. You know I run a women's magazine, and I can tell you that would never make a story. There ought to be another man or woman in it. Had you a career to go back to?'

'No. Obviously I didn't think it through. But when I told Sam I wanted to get away for a time, he said he had been having an affair with a woman, a friend of mine, in the village.'

'The biter bit.'

Beth nodded. 'Yes, I'm still reeling from the shock.'

'It strikes me you'll have to sit down and do a bit of thinking.'

'I've done that. At the back of my mind the idea was to have a holiday on my own and then go back home. You can imagine how surprised I was when Sam told me.'

'You're not used, in your neck of the woods, to husbands and wives having affairs?'

'No. At least I wasn't. You see, I thought our marriage was a very special one.'

'And yet you wanted to get away from it? Yes, you'll have to sit down and do some more thinking. I've a feeling that if you spoke to Laurel that's what she'd tell you to do. How do you think your son will react?'

'Well, I don't know if he'll have any ideas. He's gay.'

'I didn't know that. But now that you tell me...Have you explored your own sexuality, Beth?' Her look was meaningful. 'I could give you my therapist's name.'

Beth felt her cheeks burning. Of course she was straight! 'That wasn't what it was at all.'

'Were you upset about Nicholas?'

'No, but Sam was. There's no problem since he's so far away. Had it been where we live—' The buzzer went. Lia got up.

'That'll be Joe. Excuse me.' She went to the intercom and spoke into it, then opened the door. Beth heard the sound of a lift, then a man's voice. Why, oh, why did I confide in this woman? she asked herself. A dark-haired, dark-skinned man was now in the room, smiling. He had the air of one of those old film stars, she thought, self-confident.

'Now, this is Laurel's mother, Joe,' Lia said. 'Beth Crome.'

His teeth were white in his dark face. 'But you're not at all like Laurel,' he said. 'I'm sorry! Should I apologize for that remark?'

'No, she's the beauty of the family.'

'You do yourself an injustice,' he said. 'But I can tell you she's a very valuable assistant to me. Susses out people who call, the wheat from the chaff, you know, and deals with them.' He spread his hands and laughed. 'A bright girl. Jake is lucky.'

'Don't go on, Joe,' Lia said, 'or you'll worry Beth.' She turned to her. 'He's a lady-killer, this man.'

'Don't worry, Mrs Crome. I wouldn't dream of competing with Jake. Besides, I'm a married man.'

'Sit down, Joe,' Lia said, 'and join us in a drink. Maddy was unable to come?'

'Unfortunately. I've explained to Laurel. She has felt off-colour all day.' He turned to Beth. 'My wife broke her back in a riding accident last year.'

'I'm so sorry.'

'The children are out running, Joe,' Lia said. 'We'll have to wait for our dinner until they come back. I hope you're not too hungry.'

'No, a bourbon would stave off the pangs if I were.'

'Help yourself. Jake left it out for you.'

Beth watched him as he walked over to the table. Handsome, but not a young figure. He must be over fifty...But that's what you are, she reminded herself.

He called from the back of the room. 'You two ladies? A freshener?'

'I should like another gin and tonic,' Beth said, surprising herself. 'I refused Jake's offer and now I'm changing my mind.'

'Don't apologize for having a drink,' Joe Galliano said, coming over and lifting her empty glass from the table beside her. 'There's nothing like one or maybe two to make things look all right. You've had a long trip. It's stressful, flying.' He brought the drinks, and sat down on a chair facing them. 'Well, it's not often I have the pleasure of sitting with two such lovely ladies. Cheers!' He raised his glass. 'Yes,' he said, looking into it, 'today was not good for Maddy. But she's thinking of coming to Sag Harbour next week. Joanne has invited us. I have to go to Long Island to see a well known painter and poet. I want to persuade him to let me put on an exhibition of his work. The trouble is, he's rich, and doesn't need the money.'

'Trouble?' Beth laughed. 'Well, I hope you're lucky. I've been invited to go to Sag Harbour too, with Jake and Laurel, so I may meet your wife there.'

'That would be a great pleasure for both

of us. I should like to ask you about some of your modern painters in England and what you think of them. Laurel says you trained her to use her eyes.'

'It wasn't difficult with the Impressionists. Anyone would love their work.'

'Don't forget they were hooted at when they were first displayed in Paris.'

'Yes, that's true. I admire the English painters, like Hitchens, but I'm lost with the really modern, as most people of my generation are.'

There was the noise of the lift, then the door opened and Jake and Laurel burst into the room. They were both pink-cheeked. 'Here we are!' they chorused. They shook hands with Joe Galliano. Laurel kissed Lia, and Jake sat on the arm of her chair, his arm round her. 'Had a good day, Mother?' He looked at the others. 'Works herself into the ground, this woman.' Beth, looking at her, thought she suddenly did look old. Was that the result of leaving one's husband and having no one to care for you, chivvy you when you felt low? 'Drink up your vodka and have another,' he said to his mother.

'Stop fussing. No, thanks, one is my limit.' Beth looked at her own glass, half full.

'Your guests are all hungry, Laurel darling,' he said. She was deep in conversation with Joe Galliano.

'Yes, of course. Talking business.' She jumped up. 'I'll just have a quick shower and serve it. Everything is ready.' She got up and went into their room.

'I think you should join her,' Lia said to Jake. 'I don't like the wafts of East River floating around me. On you go!' She looked at Beth and Joe Galliano. 'I hope you're both not too hungry.'

'Not at all,' Beth said. She would have liked to help Laurel.

'I'm still enjoying my bourbon,' Joe Galliano said, smiling.

They talked desultorily until Laurel announced dinner, but Beth felt the atmosphere strange. Such formality. In England, had Laurel and Jake lived there, she would have gone into the kitchen and helped, but here she was reminded that she was a guest. Lia and Joe Galliano seemed to accept this. Oh, well, she thought, when in Rome...

Seven

It's good of you to run me home,' Lia said. 'Especially in a Porsche.'

'Don't butter me up. You have an Audi,' Joe Galliano replied.

'Yes, but it's a fag to take it out for small trips. I generally call a cab. I'm glad to have the opportunity to talk to you in private. I wanted to ask you if you could do me an article about modern art for *Barbara*. Choose your own painters, but stick to American.'

'I'd love to, Lia, but I must tell you, I don't get much time now for writing. With the gallery and Maddy, you can guess my time is pretty restricted.'

'Yes, I quite see that. And I know I can't tempt you with money. I shouldn't have mentioned it. Poor Maddy. Do you think she'll manage to go with you to Long Island?'

'I've explained to Joanne. It all depends how she feels on the morning in question. Her spirits go up and down.'

'Oh, I understand. I'll look in and see her this week. I'm meeting Laurel's mother for lunch on Wednesday. Perhaps I'll take her with me. I'll ring first, of course, and see how she is.'

'Yes, do that.' His voice sounded tired, she thought.

'I shouldn't be asking favours about an article when you have so much on your plate. Forget it, Joe.'

'A thought has just come into my head. This man I'm going to see at Long Island, Blaise Carey, the painter...He might write something for you, if the idea appeals. He also has a reputation in Sag Harbour of being a ladykiller. I'll have a word with him.'

'That would be fine. What did you think of Laurel's mother, by the way?'

'Distinguished, but repressed. She has style but doesn't know it.'

'I've just had an idea too. She's thinking of

leaving her husband. She didn't say so, in so many words, but I guessed it. Can you imagine, there isn't another man involved! She can't bear the thought of old age creeping up on her, and meeting it with Sam –that's her husband.'

'Did she tell you that? I know you, Lia, you'll make a story out of anything.'

'No, I guessed it. She's a romantic.'

'It sounds as if she hasn't had much worry in her life. He seemed an equable sort of chap. I spoke to him at Laurel's wedding.'

'Maybe she's thinking she's missing out on something, and needs to find out before it's too late. What about you taking her to meet Blaise Carey if, as you say, he's a ladies' man? He might fall for her.'

'I'm not a matchmaker, Lia.'

'But she needs to get about, appreciate that a bird in the hand is worth two in the bush.'

'You're incorrigible,' he said.

'That's what makes me a good editor.'

'You're right.'

'Is he one of the Summer People?' Lia asked.

'Summer People?'

'It's Joanne's name for the crowd who socialize together there – artists, poets, hangers-on. They come from New York like a flock of birds, alight at Sag Harbour. Hilde Barube, a middle-aged resident, is the queen, or rather the parties are held in her palatial home.' She guyed the word 'palatial'. 'Blaise Carey could be used as a bait. I was invited once, and that was something! Joanne and Bob have no time for her.'

'I don't blame them. Still, I might take Laurel's mother along with me if I get an invitation. Show her life as it's lived in Long Island, if Maddy doesn't come with me.'

'It's just an idea, and I hope Maddy does come along. My feeling is that Beth Crome needs to have her eyes opened. Perhaps she would realize then how lucky she is.'

'You didn't realize that when you left Bob.'

'Ah, but she and I wanted different things from our marriages. I'm sure she feels buried in the hills where she lives, whereas I had a life of my own in New York with my magazine.'

'You're a schemer, Lia. You've chosen the

right thing for you. You're in love with that magazine of yours. By the way, why did you call it *Barbara*?'

'Don't probe into my psyche, Joe.'

'OK. Your brain works like a whirlwind. Whatever underlies it, you've chosen the right thing for you. Marriage wasn't your thing, and Bob now has someone in Joanne who will be quite content to grow old with him.'

'But I've got three children out of it. When I'm old, I'm relying on them to be a comfort to me. I do dread old age. Everyone does – and death. The idea appals me. Don't you dread old age, Joe?'

'No, I intend to buy a villa in Tuscany and settle there with Maddy. If she can rest her eyes on its beauty all the time, it might help her. Besides, she's a Catholic. She might take comfort from the Church there. Religion is so much more important.'

'She might find a nice, sympathetic priest. Have you any relatives in northern Italy?'

'Yes, several brothers and sisters scattered about Bologna, Cortona, Lucca. That's where my mother lives. She's getting on for ninety, and she would like to see me before she dies.'

'Mine died in Yonkers, and I wasn't there.' Lia's voice broke. 'Now I'm feeling sorry for myself.'

'It won't last,' he said decisively, drawing into the kerb. And then, 'How on earth did you manage to get an apartment in Madison Avenue?'

'It comes with the magazine. Thank you so much, Joe, dear, for bringing me home. Would you like to come up for a last drink?'

'No, thanks. I have to get back to Maddy.'

'Of course. Give her my love.' She kissed his cheek, then got out with a sweep of her coat. 'Arrivederci!'

'Arrivederci.' He pulled away from the kerb.

'Thank you so much for a delicious meal,' Beth said. 'New York seems to be full of delightful restaurants. Laurel took me to one near her gallery.'

'Was it Greek?'

'Yes. Fascinating waiters.'

Lia Harvey was driving her towards Joe's

home to see Maddy, his wife. Lia had telephoned, and Maddy had said, yes, she would like to meet someone from England. On the way, Lia filled Beth in about Maddy and Joe.

'He was married to Bella, a quietly dignified Italian lady about his own age. They met Maddy's family through their interest in art – both families Jewish, of course – and to begin with it was Maddy's father and mother they fraternized with. Then suddenly, it seemed, he was dating Madeline, as they called her, their daughter. There was general disapproval, but it was as if they had been bewitched by each other. Bella divorced him, and he and Maddy married. It was a quiet wedding, because I think there were so many people who were voicing their disapproval, including Joe's children, and especially Maddy's parents. Then the blow fell. Her passion was riding, and three months after they were married, she was thrown from her horse and broke her back. You can imagine how everyone felt, including her parents. The rumour went that she had been pregnant. Well, Joe has been magnificent. He looks after her, he has made his peace with her parents and has been a truly devoted husband. When you think, Beth, he must have married her for sex, as much as anything else, it was a bitter blow. Needless to say, she can't have children now, but he has two sons and a daughter by Bella, and as they are more of Maddy's age, they have rallied round. In a way, her accident has healed the rift.' Lia gestured. 'Brooklyn Heights. This is where Joe's house is. It was his father's place, and he moved in here before it became as desirable as it is now. These are called walk-up brownstones, and it's considered elegant to live here now.' Beth, looking around, could see by the facades that it was impressive. Lia stopped at one of the houses. 'And here we are. It used to be where all the people who mattered lived, but the moneyed ones have moved up the river, or to the Upper East Side. Shall we get out?'

They negotiated a flight of steps, Beth thinking that however impressive the house was, it was unsuitable for an invalid. Her own house, where anyone could be pushed into the garden in a wheelchair, if necessary, and have lovely views all round, would have been more suitable.

A smart young maid answered the door when Lia had rung the bell, and ushered them in. She led them up an imposing flight of stairs and stopped at a door. There was the sound of jazz music coming from inside. The maid knocked and opened the door. 'Visitors for you, Mrs Galliano,' Beth heard her say. She stood aside to let them enter.

A young woman was seated at the window in a wheelchair with a white cat on her lap. Beth had mistaken it at first for some sort of fur cover, because it was so inanimate. 'Turn off the music, Maria,' the girl said to the maid. She held out her arms to Lia. 'Lia! How lovely to see you! And you've brought Laurel's mother. How nice!' She held out a hand to Beth. 'Your daughter is a friend of mine. What shall I call you?'

'Beth, please.' She bent down, holding the girl's hand, and kissed her cheek. What was there to say? 'What a lovely cat!' She stroked its back, and its head moved. Thank goodness it's real, she thought.

'She's called Snowball. My faithful companion. Never leaves me.'

'I'm so glad to meet you. I met your husband at Laurel's the other night.'

'And I suppose Lia filled you in about me while she drove you here?' She had dancing black eyes, and black hair tied back from her face. She was obviously young, about Laurel's age, but there were lines round her fine eyes and her face was lean with prominent cheekbones.

Beth said, 'She was telling me how well you coped. And you have your music, which is good.'

'Except that I can't dance. May I give you something to drink?'

'Thank you. I'll have what you usually have around this time.'

'Lia?'

'One of your delicious cocktails, please. I've never known the recipe, but I can swear by them, Beth.'

'I'm not giving you my recipe, Lia,' the girl said. 'You'd print it in *Barbara*.'

'I'd love to, if you gave me permission.'

'No, I have to have my secrets. Maria,' she

said to the maid who was standing at the door. 'Bring three cocktails, please.'

'Yes, Mrs Galliano.' She went away.

'Would you like to be downstairs?' Maddy said to Lia and Beth. 'I didn't feel like going down this morning. Joe had a lift put in, so it's quite easy. I'm in one of my retreating moods, so I'm glad you have both come.'

'It's a delightful room,' Beth said. 'And a lovely view. It's like being on top of the world.' She crossed to look out of the window.

'Yes, I feel like a bird up here, as if I could take off and fly over Manhattan, and see all the streets I used to know so well...' She stopped speaking, lowered her head, then raised it, pushing back her dark hair. 'So what are you up to these days, Lia?' she said.

'I may be joining the exodus to Sag Harbour, to Joanne and Bob's place. But I have to remember it's no longer mine. Beth's going. And so are you, aren't you, Maddy?'

'I hope so. But lately I haven't felt like going out. Do you know the feeling, Beth? Do you have a round of gaiety where you live in England?'

'I live in a remote part of it,' Beth said. 'Surrounded by mountains.' She was going to say 'cut off', but how could she complain, seeing this girl imprisoned? 'Yes, we do have a lot of invitations, perhaps because of our situation, and we all make a great effort to entertain, and drive a considerable distance to reach each other's houses. I was brought up in Maidstone in Kent, where everyone was accessible.'

'Which do you prefer? No, don't answer that, it's not fair. Do you have any pictures of where you live?'

'The Lakes? Not with me, but I could promise to send you some photographs we have at home. My son, Nicholas, is a very fine photographer, and I'm sure there are plenty in the house.'

'That would be lovely. I should like to live in a place like your Lakes; I grow weary of the scenery here. I used to get out of the city and ride in upstate New York, but...' She shrugged. 'I meant to travel such a lot.'

'Get Joe to take you about, Maddy. Arrangements are made for...' Lia stopped short.

'Cripples like me?'

'Let's say, disadvantaged. I had an article in the magazine last week about a young woman like you, who had done a world trip with her husband.'

'Well, good for her. But no one who is normal has any idea of the accoutrements one needs when embarking on a trip, even if it's as near as Sag Harbour. There's—'

'Stop, Maddy! I know it all, because you've told me. I know it's no comparison, but look at Beth. She's just crossed the Atlantic, and seemed to find it quite easy.' Maddy turned to look at Beth.

'Didn't your husband want to go with you?' she asked.

'It wasn't that. But I planned the trip for myself, to be alone, to contemplate...'

'Doesn't your marriage suit you?'

Beth glanced at Lia.

'Go on, answer her,' Lia said. 'This is typical Maddy. She thinks she can ask any questions she likes when she's sitting in that wheelchair.'

'Truthfully, then, I had forgotten what it

was like to be truly independent, and wanted to experience it again.'

'Was your husband unfaithful to you?'

Beth flushed. 'Do I have to answer that?'

'No, because I can see he was. I'm in a position to tell you that it doesn't matter a damn.' There was a knock at the door. 'Come in, Maria,' she said, smiling mischievously at Lia and Beth.

The girl came in carrying a tray with three glasses on it and distributed them around.

'Tell me what you think,' Maddy said to Beth, 'about your cocktail.'

Beth sipped. It was very pleasing, with a strong flavour of ginger, and mango, she thought. 'I'm a tyro where cocktails are concerned. We just go in for gin and Italian wine, or just tonic.'

'You're quite modern in the Lakes. This is called Maddy's: ginger, mango, pawpaw and a good dash of gin. The danger is that sitting here, I could become an old toper. But Joe keeps an eye on me.'

'Who could blame you?' Lia said.

'Now, where were we?' Maddy looked at both of them.

'I think you were interrogating me,' Beth said, 'like a village bobby.'

'Bobby?'

'Policeman.'

'Now I'm learning something. Thanks, Beth.' The three of them laughed. 'I should apologize, but I get so bored sitting in this chair that I play games. The only one to criticize is Snowball. She just turns her head and looks at me when I say anything too outrageous. Oh, I've just remembered what I was going to say to you, Beth.' She took a sip from her glass. 'It was that from the depth of my experience, I think couples place too much emphasis on sex. If a man misbehaves, the woman either runs away or pays him back by taking a lover herself. But in our case, Joe's and mine, because of my accident we have built up a much stronger bond than one would have thought possible.'

'Well, there's nothing to gainsay there,' Lia said. There was a pause.

'Come on, Beth,' Maddy said. 'Let's hear your opinion.'

'I think you've got a point. I must say I've

missed Sam since I left him, if I'm being honest, but it's because I had got used to having him around, operating as a twosome. But it's still nice to be a complete person on one's own, to appreciate things, form one's own opinion, not forever be comparing notes as if I couldn't think for myself.'

'Give it time,' Maddy said. She bent over Snowball, stroking the cat's fur. 'Snowball hasn't an opinion here. She's been spayed. Just as I have, through force of circumstances. I would say, if you go on thinking like that, you should never have married in the first place.' Beth thought, but she has never known the taboos which existed for the young in my day, and how we all rushed into marriage, but Maddy interrupted her thoughts. 'Are you enjoying your "Maddy", Beth?'

She was nonplussed for a moment then, holding up her glass, she said, 'I must have. See. I've emptied this!'

'Well, we must have another.'

'No, no,' Lia said. 'We've had enough of your elixir. Have mercy on the driver. How am I going to drive over Brooklyn Bridge without running into something?'

'True. That's what I miss, driving. Speeding out of New York along by the Hudson to where I used to ride. Do you ride in the Lakes, Beth?'

'No, but the children did. They had sturdy little Lakeland ponies.'

'I think we must be going,' Lia said, getting up. 'We don't want to tire you.'

'That's what everyone says, just when I'm beginning to enjoy myself. I was going to give you another cocktail, and we should have laughed together, and Beth would have told me about the Lakes in England, and I should have been transported there...'

'I'd be happy to come back again,' Beth said. 'But I hope we'll meet again at Sag Harbour.'

'I'll try to come, to please Joe.'

'They're going, Snowball.' Maddy bent over the huge cat. 'Wave a paw.' She lifted the cat's foreleg and shook it about. 'Bye-bye, people, come again soon, to see poor Maddy.'

In the car, Lia said, 'I thought we'd better leave before she became maudlin. It's such a pity, she's beginning to use drink as a solace. Joe's very worried about it.'

'And she plays games with people. You can't blame her. Such a lovely girl!' She hoped Maddy kept her wits, or there would be more to worry about than her accident.

Lia drove Beth back to Laurel and Jake's flat, saying she had to get back to *Barbara*.

The flat looked very empty. Faced with a long afternoon ahead, Beth went into her bedroom, took off the suit she had been wearing, kicked off her shoes, and lay down on the bed. She wanted to think, to turn over in her mind what Maddy had said.

Eight

Sam and Mary were in his car driving towards Ambleside. They both needed plants for their gardens, and they had agreed that they should visit the garden centre there, and then she would come back to his house for a meal. It was better that they shouldn't be seen eating out together, she had said, and he had agreed. Buying plants together was an innocent pursuit.

On their way back from what Sam had called 'a stately pleasure dome', remembering how the centre had grown from a simple place to buy plants, to a towering glass edifice, Mary asked him, 'Have you heard from Beth?'

'Yes,' he told her. 'She phoned me when she arrived. She's going with Jake and Laurel to a place called Sag Harbour in

129

Long Island, where his parents have a summer house. It was arranged before she went. We visited the Stansbys there on our first visit. Very quaint, but reeks of money. It was once a whaling harbour, and in the little town there's a museum, quaint shops, it's full of atmosphere. I hesitate to call it a village. On the outskirts it seems deserted, no one walking about. Sand everywhere. I expect they stick to their gardens. The house is quaint too, and you just cross the road to the sea.'

'They seem to live in quite a style, Laurel's in-laws.'

'Yes, she's lucky. Her husband, Jake, is in the firm with his father, Bob Stansby. Beth says Laurel has completely changed – soignée, I think the word would be. Anyhow, she's fallen on her feet.'

'You and Beth always fussed too much about your children.'

He looked at her. 'Did you think so?'

'Yes, we just sat back and let our two get on with it.' Sam thought she sounded smug, but it was true. Rachel and William Cass had caused no trouble, had married and settled down and produced grandchildren. 'Smug' was the word Beth had used for the Casses, but Mary had been right. They, or rather Beth, had endlessly fussed about Laurel when she was in London. And perhaps he'd shown his disappointment when Nicholas dropped out of university.

Mary praised his cooking, and after they had coffee she told him to sit down and rest and she would wash up. When he went into the kitchen with the coffee cups he saw she had totally different ways of clearing up than Beth, and had rinsed and stacked the plates and put the knives in a jug of hot water. She said, he thought aggrievedly, 'I thought you'd have a dishwasher, Sam.'

'No, Beth never wanted one, and when we had parties we always had Jenny from the cottages to wash up. She also helped Beth with preparing food, vegetables, and so on, set the table, and she could make wonderful party nibbles. Beth said she was invaluable, and she would rather pay Jenny than have a dishwasher.'

He saw Mary's look, and thought, I must not go on about what Beth did or thought.

'Would you like to stay tonight, Mary?' he said.

'Do you want me to?'

'I'd be very happy if you would.' How true is that? he wondered. Are you asking her because you think she expects it?

'If it made me feel more at ease in your house, I'd like to. I feel Beth's presence very strongly.'

'She suggested me going to you. She shouldn't have left me the way she did, wondering...'

'Let's go and plant your chrysanths. It's still light. Then I'll make up my mind.'

'Fair enough.' He could understand her dilemma. It was the same for him, and now there was this other thing that was bothering him. 'We'd better start before it's dark. We'll have to go to the shed first for compost, then get the plants. They're round the back of the house.' Strange, he thought, to do some gardening as a prelude to seduction.

They worked together, and he liked how a curl of blonde hair escaped and lay across her eyes, and how she kept blowing it away.

He also liked how she had difficulty getting up from kneeling like he did, and how he had to get the kneeler for her.

'It's terrible, isn't it?' she said. 'When your legs won't work for you.'

'Try this kneeler. I use it constantly. I was just showing off.'

When they went back into the house, it had become dark, and Sam lit the fire which he had set with apple wood – an old tree which he'd sawn down. He was proud of his pile of firewood.

'Do you miss her?' Mary said. They were sitting on the sofa in front of the fire.

'Not during the day, I have so many things to see to, and in bed, well...' He couldn't explain to Mary how desire seemed to have left him, because that would make her think he didn't want her. But he did, or at least, he wanted someone to be beside him and comfort him. Beth had never been like that. Bed for her had been for two things only, making love and sleeping – to lie comfortably together had never been her thing. She preferred to listen to the radio, or read a book, which necessitated the bedside light being on.

He didn't think his lack of desire was to do with Beth or Mary; it wasn't something you could discuss with a woman. Or a doctor, however well you knew him. He still baulked at the idea. Still, he and Mary had had that night together, and that had been all right. What did that prove? Was this constant feeling of fatigue anything to do with it? He hadn't mentioned it to Beth and he wasn't going to mention it to Mary. Women were offended so easily. What the hell, he thought, here goes...

He put his arm round her, and she turned her face to him, tilting it. They kissed, and that was all right.

'Neither of us are very good at this,' he said. 'What should my next move be?' He laughed. 'I feel like a boy on his first date.'

'A drink, I should think. What about a brandy?'

'Brilliant.' He got up and poured two tots, gave her one, and put his on the table. 'Back in a moment.' In the downstairs toilet he made up his mind. He would make an appointment with Alan Barclay tomorrow.

'You look tired, Sam,' she said when he came back.

'Me? Tired? Not on your life.' But he was. This dreadful fatigue...

'Well, knock that back and see how you feel.' All he felt was an overwhelming desire to drop into bed, with or without her. He felt her eyes on him.

'Great!' he said. He got up, held out his hands to her and pulled her to her feet.

'Not in yours and Beth's room,' Mary said.

'No? The trouble is the other bedrooms all have twin beds, or single beds.'

'Well, what's wrong with this?' She pointed to the rug in front of the fire.

'Nothing at all!' He forced some bonhomie into his voice. He flung down some cushions from the sofa, and pulled her down with him. In the firelight he thought she looked beautiful. At least, her complexion seemed to reflect the light on it and looked like the inside of a shell. That was because she was fair, of course, he told himself. He remembered how, in the early days of his marriage, he and Beth had done the same thing. That and the firelight seemed to do the trick. She was a very loving woman, soft to the touch.

Alan Barclay was understanding and matter-of-fact when he explained his problem. 'You don't have to feel embarrassed, Sam. I've seen most of my friends with their trousers down. And you may have nothing to worry about. You were wise to come and see me, nevertheless. As regards the symptoms you've described to me, they could be anything or nothing, but to make sure I'm going to send you to a urologist.'

'What would he be looking for?'

Alan met his eyes. 'Prostate cancer. It must have crossed your mind. You're a bit young for it, but anyone over fifty is at risk.'

'What will he do?'

'First, a simple urine test and a PSA. That's essential for early detection. You have to prepare yourself for lots of hanging around with appointments, and so on. By the way, your urologist will certainly carry out a DRE, but you're not going to object to that, I'm sure.'

'Come on, Alan. Spill the beans. What on earth's that?'

'Examining you rectally. If there is anything to worry about, he may have to perform a biopsy. I'm giving you the whole works, but tell yourself it won't reach that stage. I don't think you're a worrier, are you?'

'Not until now.'

'Take Beth into your confidence.'

'She's left me,' he said, and wanted to cry. Then, seeing Alan's shocked expression, he said, 'Not really, she's gone off on a jaunt on her own to see the children. I think she got fed up with me in bed.'

'You should have come clean with her, and come to see me earlier.'

'Will it make any difference?'

'No, I don't think so. We'll get appointments made. I know a good man in Kendal whom you can see. Depending on what he finds, he may adopt the watch-and-wait technique, and if you take my advice, you should phone Beth and put her in the picture. It's a good thing you haven't moved in a floozy in her place. Your feeling of fatigue is probably due to worry. You could have saved yourself that...'

'Yes, I see that now. But I suppose I'm like most men. You expect to carry on carrying on without any trouble.'

Alan Barclay got to his feet. 'I always find it better to spell it out, and I know you as a sensible man. Take my advice and ring Beth and tell her.'

Nine

Beth was sitting with Bob and Joanne on the wide terrace in front of the Stansbys' house in Sag Harbour. She looked over the garden, its lawns and flowerbeds towards the blue Sound with its strip of white sand. Idyllic, she thought, although Joanne complained about the sand. Beth had gathered she was very house-proud. 'It gets everywhere,' she had said. Anyone who walked about outside, in the drive or on the shore, were asked to empty their shoes before they entered the house. 'Dora complains,' she had apologized, 'about her floors.' Dora was the housekeeper, not at all the fearsome creature one would have thought, but a youngish woman who came with the Stansbys from the Riverdale house.

If Beth had been impressed with the

Riverdale house, she was even more so with this one. She and Sam had liked it better. It was smaller than the New York one, with old, well-worn furniture, American Provincial, Dutch-tiled stoves, bobble-edged chenille covers on tables, antimacassars on chair backs, even a ship's bell at the door. It was full of character. Bob had told them he had inherited it from his parents. It was generally filled with flowers by Joanne, who, it seemed, spent a part of each morning in the flower room. It was difficult not to be impressed by a house that had a special room for arranging flowers, with its sinks, stone floor, shelves for vases, scissors, secateurs – all the accoutrements necessary for such a task. Sam, too, had been impressed, as one who apprecated his own garden shed so much, and where he trimmed bunches of flowers and presented them to Beth, ready for arranging. She had always looked forward to his first cutting of sweet peas, with their delicate fragrance.

Joanne said, 'The children have gone down to torment Jake and Laurel.'

'It's time they were here.' Bob Stansby

looked at his watch. 'They've missed breakfast.'

'Don't you remember?' His wife looked at
him. 'Laurel said she would be cooking
breakfast for them in the cottage. She and
Jake still like playing at houses.'

'Here they come!' He interrupted her.
'But not with the children.' He waved, and
Beth saw Laurel and Jake walking towards
the house. You had to stay with people to
discover their temperaments, she thought.
Joanne was house-proud, Bob was tetchy.

'They make a lovely couple,' Joanne said.
'Don't you think so, Beth?'

'I do.' She had been thinking the same
thing, and once again felt thankful that
Laurel had met Jake in Hong Kong. Laurel
was wearing a sundress, her arms and legs
bare and brown, and Jake had on a black tee
shirt and white trousers. He had his arm
round her shoulders. To avoid overenthus-
ing, she asked, 'Where are Betsy and Maybelle?'

'They'll have gone to look for Uncle Joe,
as they call him. The first thing he does
when he comes here is to get into the sea.

He says it's not like the Ligurian coast, but it's got to do.'

'Do you like swimming, Beth?' Bob asked.

'I do, immensely. But I'm a coward. It takes me about three days to coax myself to go in. Swimming pools are best for me. Someone can push me in there.'

'Well, Joanne and I go to the pool before lunch. Perhaps you'd like to join us?'

'Thank you. I'd love that. And I'll give you the pleasure of pushing me in.'

'Here we are!' Jake said, announcing themselves as he and Laurel came up the stone stairs to the terrace. 'This dearly beloved of mine took ages to cook breakfast. I thought we'd never get here.'

'Don't believe him,' Laurel laughed, punching Jake on the shoulder. 'He wouldn't get out of bed. It took Betsy and Maybelle ages to pull the bedclothes off him, lazy devil.'

'Now that you're here,' Bob Stansby said, 'do you want to go to the Barube party tonight? I'd like to call her back, although she says it's open house.'

'Shall we?' Jake turned to Laurel. 'You'll

meet all the locals.'

'Joe said this morning that he was going,' his father said. 'You might like to accompany him, Beth?' Maddy hadn't come with him after all, Beth thought.

'We shan't be going,' Joanne said. 'We call her and the crowd she collects round her the Summer People. When they come here, mostly from the city, they have endless parties. Invitations fly about. There's endless competition, but it doesn't appeal to us.'

'I'd like to go,' Beth said.

'You're Summer People too, Joanne.' Jake smiled at her.

'Shhh!' she said, putting a finger to her lips.

Beth caught sight of Joe Galliano in a white robe walking across the grass, with the two little girls skipping along on either side of him. 'Perhaps we could ask Mr Galliano if he's willing to escort me?' Beth said. 'Here he comes. His wife has been unable to come, then?'

'Yes, unfortunately,' Bob said. 'He arrived late last night on his own. I think Maddy dreads travelling.'

'Mother has met Joe at our apartment,' Laurel said. 'And you went to see Maddy, didn't you, with Lia?' She asked Beth.

'Yes. She said she was hoping to come here.' She wasn't surprised that Maddy hadn't joined the party. She hadn't looked well enough to make the effort.

'Come along, Joe,' Jake called to him as he was walking up the terrace steps. 'You're going to Miss Barube's tonight, aren't you? Beth is looking for an escort.'

'Delighted.' And to Beth, 'As a matter of fact, I intended to ask you, Beth, but I arrived late last night and breakfasted before you, then went for a swim.'

'Maddy isn't here, I've heard. I'm so sorry. Unlike you, Joe, I slept in. It must be the good air here. Yes, I'd love to go to the party.'

'My mother called it good bleaching air, I remember,' Bob said. 'Clothes worn around here tend to have a washed-out look. At least it hasn't been polluted, like New York.'

'As a matter of fact,' Joe Galliano said, 'I have a special reason for going to the party. I called Blaise Carey last night to see if we could meet while I was here, and he suggested Miss Barube's house as a venue, as he was going to be there.'

'He's one of that crowd,' Joanne said. 'The women adore him.'

'He's a good painter,' Bob said.

'He is,' Joe nodded. 'I want to persuade him to let me put on a show of his stuff in my gallery.'

'He's a nice guy. But you may have difficulty. He doesn't need the money and has steadfastly refused all offers from local galleries.'

'Well, there's no harm in trying.'

'We tried to get Jake out of bed this morning!' Betsy burst out. She and her sister were sitting on the steps. 'And he kept holding on to the bedclothes.'

'There was a reason for that, dear stepsister,' Jake said. Both little girls giggled, and put their hands to their mouths.

'And then we went down to the shore and watched Mr Galliano swimming,' Maybelle said.

'Like a whale,' her sister said. 'That's what you said, Maybelle.'

'Girls!' Joanne said, laughing with the rest. 'That's rude, and you know it's rude!'

'Don't scold them,' Joe said. 'It's probably near the mark. I'm the one who got away at Montauk, girls. Hadn't you heard?'

Sam liked this place, Beth thought, when she was dressing for the party. She had swum in the pool with Bob and Joanne, and then, with Joe, had watched Laurel and Jake playing a strenuous game of tennis. Afterwards, lunch was served outside, and they'd all gone to Sag Harbour to shop, followed by tea in a cafe, where everyone seemed to know everyone else. Sam had liked Sag Harbour and the Stansbys' house. He hadn't been envious. He had always been satisfied with their own house, with his life and their friends...Until she had spoiled it, she thought. Laurel was the right age for all this. She would develop into a New York matron, like Joanne. And Jake's right for her. He would be a good husband, but he might fall into the rich person's pattern of life here, with extramarital affairs when marriage palled. You, she thought, are not in a position to make criticisms. You've left Sam, albeit temporarily.

She sat down to ring Nicholas, having previously asked Joanne if she might do so. In a few minutes she heard his voice.

'Nicholas, it's Mother here. I'm staying with Laurel's in-laws in Long Island. I've booked to fly to Hong Kong a week on Monday, the twenty-third of September. I don't want to overstay my welcome here. Is that all right?'

'Perfectly. I'll come to the airport to meet you. Do you know the time of your arrival?'

'Yes, I have it here.' She read from the ticket which she had lying on the table in front of her.

'Are you enjoying yourself?'

'Very much. A bit overpowering, the people I mean, their way of life. We've driven here from New York.'

'We have a lot of Americans here. A tremendous zest for life. I know what you mean. Mother, I'll book you into a hotel near us.' It couldn't be plainer.

'There's no need. Couldn't I stay with you?'

'It's a tiny flat.' He sounded doubtful. 'But you can use it during the day, if you like.'

'Are you sure you want me there?'

'Of course. I'm looking forward to seeing you, and to hearing all about Dad, and your adventures in New York.'

'I'm getting ready for a party tonight.'

'Don't let it go to your head.' She thought he sounded amused and patronizing – rather like Laurel, who sometimes looked at her as if this was someone she didn't know. She must have a frank talk with her before she left.

Joe was waiting in the sitting room for her. Joanne and Bob were there too. He got up when she came into the room.

'Oh how nice you look, Beth,' he said. 'Doesn't she?' he appealed to Bob and Joanne, who nodded approvingly.

'Very elegant. Don't let that crowd sweep you off your feet,' Joanne said.

'Would you rather I didn't go?'

'No, not at all. You're doing us a favour, representing us. It's just that Bob and I value our privacy, and don't want to get swept into that crowd. We come here to relax, and enjoy our family and friends. It's a pity your husband isn't with you.'

'I'm acting as his stand-in,' Joe said.

'Well, off you go,' Bob said. 'Jake and Laurel will be leaving from the cottage. He always drives from New York so that he can have his car here. I can no longer face that expressway, so I keep one here.'

'I hate to say this,' Joe said when they were driving to Miss Barube's house, 'but Joanne and Bob are getting set in their ways. I think his marriage to Lia made him long for the quieter life.'

'Perhaps I should have stayed with them?'

'No, they'll be glad we're going to stand in for them. And I have this appointment to meet Blaise Carey.'

'Yes, you have a reason. I'm just curious to see how life is lived here. Local colour.' She laughed.

'They're like a lot of hummingbirds, bright colours, endless chatter. No wonder Bob and Joanne get tired of them. Bob says it's like a monkey house.'

As he drove up the drive, they could hear

the noise of a jazz band. The windows were wide open, and Beth saw people dancing inside. 'Like *The Great Gatsby*,' she said.

'But minus those wonderful songs of Cole Porter. "Begin the Beguine". Come on, Beth, it's your turn.'

'"I get a kick out of you..."' She laughed.

'Good. "I've got you under my skin..."' He sang.

They went into the house, his arm round her shoulders, and were immediately swallowed up by the dancers.

'We'll have to extricate ourselves from this,' Joe said, 'and pay our respects to Miss Barube.' They were dancing on the fringe of the crowd.

'Does she live alone?'

'As far as I know. She'll have lots of retainers. Joanne tells me that she inherited this house from her parents, and that she's trying to set up a kind of salon here.'

They made their way round the edge of the room, dancing through laughing crowds of people who were talking animatedly, some with glasses in their hands, and arrived at a sofa near the plinth where the band was playing. Joe took Beth's hand, and led her towards a sofa on which a thin, grey-haired woman was sitting, waving her cigarette holder in time to the music. She was the first person Beth had seen so far with grey hair *au naturel*. Nevertheless she was a striking woman, with a thick grey fringe above bright black eyes. Her skin was tanned, her lips a vivid red, her top teeth large and resting on her bottom lip when she wasn't talking. The people around her melted away as Joe and Beth approached her. When she raised her hand to welcome them, the grey chiffon sleeve slid up her arm, which was tanned and bony.

'Good evening, Mr Galliano,' she said. 'You've managed to tear yourself away from New York? How is your lovely young wife?'

'She's not so well at the moment, but I've brought a house guest from the Stansbys', Mrs Beth Crome, mother-in-law of Jake.'

'How do you do, Mrs Crome,' she said. 'You're very welcome. Yes, your daughter and son-in-law are here. I don't think Bob and Joanne like parties, or perhaps it's mine. Now sit down beside me, and I'll introduce you to anyone who comes along. Have you had champagne?'

'No, we haven't, Miss Barube.'

'Here's Luigi with the tray. Do help yourselves.' She looked up at a man who had stopped beside her. 'Why, hello, Blaise! I'm glad *you* haven't turned down my invitation.' He was of medium height, thin-faced, with hair swept back from his forehead and curling round his neck. He wore a paisley-patterned scarf tucked into his shirt collar.

'Hilde.' He bent down and kissed her cheek. 'Turned down? You are the doyenne of the Sag Harbour artistic crowd. As if I could miss one of your parties!' She looked mollified.

'Allow me to introduce you to Mrs Beth Crome from England. She's the mother of the Stansbys' daughter-in-law. She has such a pretty voice. I love the English intonation.'

'Mrs Crome.' They shook hands. He was fair-haired and blue-eyed, and she thought he had a washed-out appearance, perhaps caused by the same air that Bob Stansby extolled. He wasn't tanned. 'And Mr Joe Galliano, from New York,' Hilde

Barube said.

'Ah, we meet, Mr Galliano.' He smiled and shook hands. 'How convenient.'

'Extremely,' Joe said. He turned to Hilde Barube. 'Mr Carey said he would be here tonight. I hope you won't mind if we use your house for a little business discussion.'

'If you're trying to get him to sell some pictures to you,' she said, 'I'm afraid you're wasting your time.'

'You're naughty, Hilde,' Blaise Carey said. 'You've just made that up.'

'I hope she has.' Joe smiled. 'But I don't mind if you want to keep your celebrities in Sag Harbour. It's only his pictures I'm interested in. You don't mind if I whisk him away?'

'Ply him with champagne,' Hilde Barube said, her black eyes dancing, her prominent teeth showing. 'Off you go then. Mrs Crome is going to sit and listen to my gossip, and I'm going to listen to her voice.'

There was little chance for gossip, what with the noise of people laughing and talking, the music of the band, and every now and then someone stopping to talk to Hilde

Barube. Beth was constantly introduced to different people, who stayed to talk and then drifted away again.

'Fortunately,' her hostess said, 'you have just met the lion of my party, Blaise Carey. He's very popular here. And generous with his money.'

'Is there a Mrs Carey?'

'There was. I'm afraid that's the state of affairs here. I've never married. My parents owned this house, and when they both died I decided to have lots of parties to make up for the miserable childhood I had with them. I once thought I was going to be a painter, and had no time for men. If I could have painted like Blaise, I shouldn't be having parties, but, alas, it was a mediocre talent.'

'Do you still paint, Miss Barube?'

'Hilde, please. No, I gave it up. I was disappointed in myself when I saw the work around me. When Mama and Papa died I went off to Paris to study, but dropped it to enjoy life there. I let myself go, which was a great mistake.' She turned to Beth. 'One should never step out of character. I should have stayed in New York and taken a job like your daughter's. I knew about paintings, and who knows, I might have met someone who was attracted to me and wanted to marry. It is my great regret. I enjoy othcr people marrying, and divorcing, the whole spectacle. I had no brothers or sisters to talk to, just two parents who practically kept me under lock and key. Naturally the house was left to me.' Beth saw the black eyes were serious now. 'It's not often I let my hair down, but it's easy with you. You're not American, which makes me feel safe. Now you must tell me about yourself. Fair exchange!'

'I've left my husband, temporarily, and am visiting my two children...'

'Then...?'

'I simply don't know. It's good for me being in an entirely different place and with entirely different people. I can see myself. Do you know what I mean?'

'To stand outside yourself? Yes, I know. Is your husband long-suffering?'

'He's equable. I think that's the word for him. And content with life.'

155

'But it's people who aren't like that who get things done. I should watch your step, Beth.' She gave her a penetrating look. 'Enough of confidences. Let's go and have something to eat. I expect you're thinking I am lucky, whereas I think *you* are. Come along, I'll introduce you to more guests. You may find our two lost men in the dining room. Men talk better round a table.'

The band had stopped playing but the noise had scarcely abated. The chatter and laughter hit Beth as they entered the large room. It was seething with people, and she heard isolated voices calling out when they appeared. 'Lovely party, Hilde!' 'Gorgeous food!' 'Come and sit with us!' She moved between the tables like a queen, shaking hands, smiling, occasionally introducing Beth to various people, and when they sat down it was because of a chorus of appeals from a large noisy party who seemed to know each other, making her feel out of place. Fortunately, Laurel and Jake were at the same table, next to where she had squeezed in on Hilde's command.

'Are you enjoying yourself, Beth?' Jake

asked her.

'Yes, thank you. I've been dropped by Joe, I think. He went off with Blaise Carey.'

'He's angling for Carey.'

'I think he's very attractive,' Laurel said. 'I bet Mum did too.'

'There's no reason why I shouldn't.' Something was annoying Laurel, she thought. Does she feel I've stepped out of my role, and is worried that I have left Sam at home? Or perhaps that I'm muscling in on her territory? 'You and I will have to have lunch together before I catch the plane to Hong Kong,' she said. 'I called Nicholas tonight. Time is going so swiftly, and we hardly get time to talk.'

'Make the most of your mother, Laurel,' Jake said. 'You won't see her for a long time. And you know you miss England very much.'

'Do you, Laurel?' She turned to her.

'Yes, I didn't think I would. I think of our house often, and how it was sort of cradled in the fells, and the noise of the beck running through the garden.' Beth noticed Jake put his arm round her and draw her close to him, as if in sympathy.

'We had a favourite climb, Jake.' She turned to him. 'Langdales, it was called, and we used to slide down the slope, the four of us, into the most wonderful tea place, where they plied us with scones and delicious home-baked bread, heaps of strawberry jam, and rum butter, and gingerbread made in Grasmere. I haven't had a tea like that since I came here.'

'That's homesickness,' Beth said.

'Yes, I know. But Jake cheers me up when I'm dismal.'

'I was away from home for four years, at Yale,' he said. 'And I have to admit I missed my home too, and all the things that went with it.'

'What do you call your home?' Beth asked. 'Here or New York?'

'I think here. I spent some very happy times with my sisters, Nancy and Claire, and Lia and my father. But it fell apart. That was sad for me.'

Laurel kissed his cheek. 'But we cheer each other up, don't we?'

'Do you miss London, Laurel?' Beth

asked, thinking of the young man, Dave, who had died.

'No. Not now I have Jake. He knows.' She turned to him. They're in love, Beth thought, the way Sam and I were...She felt a lump in her throat.

Joe and Blaise Carey had appeared at her side. 'I'm so sorry for deserting you,' Joe said.

Blaise Carey said, 'I'm sure Mrs Crome has been well looked after.' His eyes met Beth's.

'Do you want to go now?' Joe asked.

'What are you doing?' she appealed to Jake.

'I think we're leaving. Laurel?'

'Yes. Would you like a lift, Mum?'

'No, that's my prerogative,' Joe said. 'We're going in the same direction.'

'Well, that's settled,' Beth said, getting up from the table with Laurel and Jake. She met Blaise Carey's eyes again and said, 'Goodbye, Mr Carey.' They shook hands. 'I've been hearing a lot about your paintings.'

'It's a gossipy place, Sag Harbour. But Joe

here has been telling me of the richer benefits of New York.' He turned to Jake and Laurel. 'Nice to see you again, Jake. You and your beautiful wife.' He shook hands with them, then turned to Joe. 'You're coming tomorrow to my studio. Why don't you bring Mrs Crome and Jake and his wife?'

'I'm afraid we have to get back to New York in the morning,' Jake said. 'Work. Both of us are minions.'

'I have to open the gallery,' Laurel said, smiling. 'Have you forgotten, Joe?'

'It wouldn't exist without you!' He laughed.

'It might be more convenient if you picked me up tomorrow morning, Jake,' Beth said. 'I could be ready.'

'But you mustn't run away without seeing my pictures, Mrs Crome,' Blaise Carey said. 'Joe would, I'm sure, give you a lift back to New York.' Beth looked doubtfully from one to the other.

'Delighted,' Joe said. 'And it gives me a chance to see your portfolio.'

'That's good of you, Joe,' Jake said, 'It will save Beth leaving at the crack of dawn. You can drop her off at our flat.'

'I feel like piggy in the middle,' Beth said.

'Not at all,' Joe said. 'And it suits everyone. Laurel will be able to open the gallery for mc, Jakc will get to work on time, and Beth will be able to sleep on in the morning.'

'Well, that's that,' Blaise Carey said. 'I shall expect you both at three o'clock tomorrow. I'm sorry you two can't come,' he said to Jake and Laurel. Beth saw a look on Laurel's face that she remembered from her early days before she went to London. A childish resentment. She hadn't grown out of it.

In Joe's car, driving back to the Stansby house, he seemed unduly silent. 'Do you really want to go to Blaise Carey's studio tomorrow?' she asked him.

'Not really, but I'm trying to do a deal. Does that sound ungracious? Besides, sometimes I grow tired of having to think of Maddy all the time. I long for some more freedom, but I'm devoted to her, and it's difficult at times. I have a guilty feeling that I've spoiled her life. She was so young when

I met her.'

Beth was surprised. 'But you mustn't think that.' Involuntarily, she put her hand on one of his on the steering wheel. He swerved into a lay-by, stopped the car, and put his arms round her. For a moment she had thought she had caused the swerve.

'You're so understanding and sweet, Beth. I feel we're both in a predicament. What we need is comfort.' He forced her head back with his and kissed her.

She pulled away. She felt shaken and guilty. 'I'm sorry, Joe,' she said. 'I didn't mean...'

'But I thought...' He laughed. 'It wouldn't do anyone any harm if we...'

So this is what Laurel was worried about, she realized. Imagine! One's daughter being wiser than oneself! That she was out of her depth here, she admitted. But you can't pretend to be an innocent, she told herself. Liaisons went on back home. She had gone around with her eyes shut. She thought of Mary and Sam...

'I've been a fool, Joe,' she said. 'I'm out of my depth. I've been living in cloud cuckoo land. There was no intention on my part to lead you on.'

'No? I gather you gave Blaise Carey the same impression as I got.'

She felt a deep flush travelling over her face, even into her armpits. She had never blushed like that before. 'What makes you say that?'

'Men's talk. I suppose it's because you're here without your husband...' He put his head in his hands. 'His idea was that I should drive you to his studio and then disappear. Say I had to go back to New York. He would drive you up later.'

'Oh, don't.' She found she was burying her head in her hands, like Joe. 'I shouldn't be allowed out alone!'

She felt his arm go round her. He was laughing. 'Don't worry. I've no intention of deserting you when we go to the studio. I'm afraid you're a victim in all this. I wasn't definite enough. I was trying to please him so that he'd let me show his pictures in my gallery.'

'Oh! Oh! I feel *terrible*, Joe.'

'Don't castigate yourself. I feel equally

bad. Forget what I said about Maddy.'

She felt tears in her eyes. But no, she was a married woman, retired...That was the critical word...She musn't weep. Instead she said, 'Aren't personal relationships the very devil?'

When she got into bed that night, she still felt miserable and ashamed. Joe had talked to her for a long time, confessing that he had had many lovers before Maddy, and that her freshness and youth had swept him away. But it had been difficult for him after her accident. Difficult for her as well, of course, but she had been able to find comfort in her church. 'Take my advice, Beth,' he said. 'Go back to your husband.'

Sleep seemed to be impossible as she remembered the evening. The party, and then in the car with Joe, when apparently she had thrown out signals of being 'available'. And to think that Blaise Carey had been given the same impression by her! No wonder Laurel had given her odd looks from time to time. 'Don't castigate yourself,' Joe had said. But that's what she was doing now. What's wrong with you, Beth? Have you forgotten the rules because you've been married so long? She understood Mary and Sam now, and freely forgave them. They had been honest. A temporary flare of lust, which at least had been genuine. *She* was the guilty party, and she continued to berate herself. The blushes came back as she imagined the conversation between Blaise Carey and Joe, nods and winks, a married woman on the loose, fair game to men like them. No doubt Laurel and Jake had been interested spectators, had talked about her.

A bird in the hand, that was Sam. She was lucky. Her mind went back to Gran Canaria and the birds there. Was it that she had felt tied down when she saw their free flight? Or was this what was called a midlife crisis? But that was for men. Was she menopausal? You know Alan Barclay warned you about taking things more easily, not to be such a perfectionist. It had become more difficult as time went on. You were always so sensible, so sure of yourself, Beth. As the blushes faded, she felt tired and fell asleep at last, wondering if Sam would want her back.

★　★　★

In the morning, she and Joe said their goodbyes and thanks to Joanne and Bob.

'Perhaps I blotted my copybook with them as well,' she said in the car, but Joe assured her that they would feel she was in safe hands with an old and trusted friend.

'*Moi*!' He laughed.

'I hope I didn't spoil your deal with Blaise Carey?' she said later. 'I tried to behave like a maiden aunt.'

'You didn't look like one. No, I'm sure you didn't spoil anything. Actually, he had been waiting for someone like me to come along. He had no intention of bequeathing his oeuvre to Sag Harbour. I hope you got something out of your visit.'

'Well,' she said, 'I liked his pictures. And I enjoyed watching his face when I said I was going back with you.'

The journey was swift and pleasant going back to New York. Joe apologized for his behaviour the night before. 'You saw me at a weak moment,' he laughed.

'Let it be a secret between us,' she said. 'I learned a valuable lesson, and I made a good friend.'

They said goodbye to each other outside the apartments on East 57th Street. He was in a hurry to get back to Maddy. They kissed. 'A chaste kiss,' Joe said.

Laurel and Jake were back from work. 'Here she is,' Jake said.

'Shall I throw in my hat first?' she asked them.

Laurel got up and threw her arms round her. 'Oh, Mum!' she said.

'What's all this?' Jake said. 'Come on, let's have a drink. What would you like, Beth?'

'A gin and tonic, please. I must go on the water wagon when I go back home.'

'Nonsense! What shall we drink to?'

'To her safe return?' Laurel said, with that smile that Beth knew so well.

Ten

Sam had bought a Dendrobium Orchid for Mary when he was at the local Sainsbury's store, surprised at how they jumped ahead of fashion and their customers' needs, and thinking how many garden centres were put out of business because of the supermarkets' perspicacity. But he bought it all the same, because it happened to be what he hadn't known he meant to buy. Did they give a degree in merchandising now? Mary had recently started cultivating orchids in her garden room, and the plant's white beauty had caught his eye.

An alternative reason was the thought that it might sweeten what he had to say to her. He had been to see the urologist, and it had all gone according to plan. Now he had been given an appointment for a biopsy.

Alan had said, 'Don't panic. Worry is the worst thing. Tell yourself it's going to be all right, and this is just a precautionary measure.'

He had decided to wait until hc got the results before telling Beth. There was no point in her going through the worry he was facing and he didn't want her to feel that she *had* to come back to him.

Mary welcomed him, and enthused about his gift. 'How generous and thoughtful of you, Sam. I haven't got this one. Isn't it lovely? I'll take good care of it. Have you had supper?'

She was good at enthusing, he thought, compared with Beth. 'Yes, I had some before I left. Mary, I can't stay tonight. I'm sorry.' He told her his white lie. 'Beth is phoning me tonight. She's flying to Hong Kong today and it's to tell me that she has arrived.'

'Oh, couldn't you telephone Nicholas from here and find out if she's there?'

'No, he's always away somewhere. He's never in.'

'She will be staying with Nicholas, though,

won't she? William always puts me up when I go to them.' Here he agreed with Beth. She had said more than once that Mary always gave the impression that her family was whiter than white compared to theirs.

He said shortly, 'She'll phone when she arrives in Hong Kong.'

They had never discussed Nick's sexuality with anyone in the village. It was their affair. He would have liked to be honest about it, but Beth didn't want people gossiping when they weren't too sure themselves.

'I can see you've made up your mind. When is she phoning?'

'Sometime after eight. I'll have to be in all evening.'

'I can't say I'm not disappointed.' She was coy. 'I've even got my most seductive nightie laid out.'

'I'm disappointed too.' He had never felt less eager in his life. But how could he be honest? And he didn't want Mary's sympathy, not at this moment. Nor did he want to take her into his confidence. He longed to tell Beth so that she could share his anxiety. Besides she was such a pragmatic person,

whereas Mary was inclined to be sentimental and weepy. He couldn't tell her that
his mind was so full of anxiety that he
couldn't think of anything else, because he
wasn't sure of her reaction, whereas he
could bet on Beth's. That was what being
married meant. One knew one's partner
through and through, having been tried and
tested in every situation.

'You look off-colour, Sam,' she said. 'Are
you missing Beth?'

That was bitchy, he thought. She sat down
beside him on the sofa, and twisted round
to kiss him on the lips. 'Would you like a
drink before you go home?'

'I wouldn't mind, but nothing too strong,
please. Have you a Sauvignon Blanc?'

'I seem to remember that brandy did the
trick last time, but yes, I'll have to open a
bottle. It won't take me a minute.'

'Let me do it.'

'No, you sit here and I'll get your drink.'
She kissed him on the cheek this time and
got up.

While she was away he spoke sternly to
himself. Look out, he warned himself. Stick

171

to your excuse. Don't get inveigled, and don't tell her your real reason. He fell into a dream-like state, thinking of Beth and how she would have invented lots of things for them to do while they were waiting for results. She had always been the one to take charge of a situation, knowing his capacity for worrying.

Mary came into the room with two glasses of wine on a tray and cheese biscuits in a china dish. 'It's no big deal,' she said, her face making it clear that she had made up her mind while she was out of the room. 'You drink this and get home for your phone call, and then phone me when you want to come again.'

'You're sweet, Mary,' he said, won over. It would be tempting to tell her the truth to see how she reacted.

They talked together, about orchids, and she told him that her son was coming to stay next week, with his wife and family, and that it would be better if he didn't come to the house then. He said he would see her before that, and put down his empty glass.

'Thanks,' he said. 'I needed that.'

'You're strange,' she said. 'I have a feeling you're going off me.'

'What nonsense!'

'I blame Beth,' she said. 'She's left you in a funny position. You don't know where you are, what to do. I believed after the first night you had fallen in love with me, but now I'm not so sure. We'll have a good talk when you come back and get things thrashed out.'

'I'll make it tomorrow evening, if that's all right. Believe me, Mary,' he said, 'I'm just as fond of you as I was, but yes, I admit that Beth has left me in a funny position. Now I'd better get off.'

It was getting dark as he drove home, and the fells were almost hidden by the mist swirling round them. The village street was deserted.

Had Beth never really adapted to the Lakes? She spoke sometimes of feeling stifled, but he could hardly understand that. He had felt stifled when he was in the south, especially in London. Too many houses, too many people, too many cars, manicured parks that were supposed to make up for the lack of real country. 'Why,' he had asked her, 'do so many people come for holidays to the Lakes?'

'You were born here,' she had pointed out. 'You've made friends with the mountains.'

He sat in the living room when he got home without putting on the light. Outside, a moth kept bashing itself against the window. A distant sheep bleated. Had she never been content here? I'm disintegrating without her, he thought. I didn't realize how much I needed her. Was I too dull for her, quite happy being buried up here, never really wanting to take trips with her? He had kept that quiet, but he had been aware of an immense relief whenever he came home to the familiar landscape he so loved. The telephone suddenly rang and he jumped up to answer it. He heard her voice.

'Sam, how are you?'

'Fine,' he said. 'How are you? Strange, I was just thinking of you.'

'Were you? I thought I'd ring and tell you that I'm flying to Hong Kong on Monday. I'm not staying with Nicholas. He's booked me in to a hotel.'

'Well,' he said, 'that's a surprise.' He had been so convinced by his white lie that he had to stop himself saying, 'But you're supposed to have arrived there today.'

'Laurel said to me that he probably felt I'd prefer not to stay with them.'

'Them?'

'He and his partner Chris. She said we hadn't been facing up to the obvious. She's changed, Sam, since she's been here. Brittle. Looking back, I preferred her the way she was.'

'She's still Laurel, our daughter. Apropos Nick, well, we knew, didn't we? We just didn't talk about it with each other. But you must respect his wishes about the hotel. After all, what difference does it make?'

'Just that I had visions of staying with him and being there for at least two weeks – that's what I've allowed for in my booking.'

His heart lifted. She was coming back. 'So have you done a lot of thinking while you've been away?'

'Yes, although there isn't much time for thinking. That's the difference between city life and ours, but I certainly couldn't live here. I don't fit in. I'm not smart, streetwise, or young enough. I had lunch with Lia – you remember, we met her at the wedding, Bob Stansby's former wife – and I asked her what kind of person she employed at her magazine. That's why she left him. To run her magazine. And her answer was "young" and, "What I need is a clean sheet. Young girls are more malleable; they haven't too many preconceived ideas." That's why Laurel has adapted so well. She'd had experience of living in a city, and she's absorbed the American culture. And yet, there was one occasion when we did get close...'

She stopped speaking for a moment, and he got the impression that she had stopped to wipe away tears. Her voice was brighter when she spoke again. 'So obviously I wouldn't fit in here, and for New York, read London, or any big city.'

She's confusing place with person, he thought. 'Don't tell me you're changing your mind about the Lakes?'

'It's peaceful, thinking back.'

'What about me? Where do I come in?'

There was another pause and then she said, 'Give me time, Sam.'

Circumstances can change opinions, he thought, but he'd wait till he got the results before telling her. It wouldn't be fair otherwise. 'I'm really glad you phoned tonight, Beth.' Don't begin to tell her how lonely you feel without her. She has to make up her mind without you influencing it.

'Are you, Sam?' Her voice was soft, so soft, that he was tempted to change his mind about telling her. 'I've been missing you.'

'I've been sitting here with the light out, missing *you...*'

'Tell me what it's like.'

'Missing you?'

'No, what can you see outside the windows?'

'Mrs Cochrane's conservatory on one side. The other side is just grey mist, but there's the sound of the beck.'

'I always wanted a garden room like Mary Cass's, but we couldn't build it because of that damned conservatory.'

'Patience. That's what we decided, remember?'

'What else?'

'It's dusk. I believe the Scots call it "the gloaming", which sounds better to me. "Roamin' in the gloamin', wi' my lassie by my side,"' he sang.

'No, please, you were told at school not to sing.'

'I might have been taking lessons for all you know. Well, the fells are looking in, and there's a leftover moth bashing itself against the front window.'

'It'll be a leftover butterfly from the buddleia.'

'I expect.'

'How is how-does-your-garden-grow Mary?'

'She asks after you.'

'I bet she does. Well, I'd better get off this line. I'm monopolizing it, and Jake does a lot of telephoning.'

'Right.' He didn't want her to go. It felt …right. He wanted to tell her about his worry. 'Right,' he said again. 'Give my love to Laurel and Jake and my best to Nick when you see him. Enjoy Hong Kong. I miss you, Beth.' There was no reply, and he hung up, wondering if he had done the right thing in not confiding in her.

It was the following evening, and Sam was at home after a successful day out that had made him feel right with himself. Everything was going to be all right. He had phoned Mary and asked if he could drop in as he had something to tell her, and he could tell by the tone of her voice that she was intrigued.

He had gone to Wetherham in the morning, after the post had arrived with no letter from the hospital, and no call from Alan Barclay, and after some successful shopping he had been cheered by the number of people whom he had met in the busy centre who had seemed genuinely pleased to see him, the elation remaining with him when he called in at the shop. The manager greeted him warmly, as did the staff, who all professed to be missing him, and said how things were not the same since he retired. He felt the same warmth when he lunched at the George, where he had his favourite roast ham and cranberry sauce, and where he met an old climbing friend with whom he reminisced happily.

'Have you ever wanted to live anywhere else, Jim?' he asked his friend.

'No, definitely not, and if I did, one visit to Friar's Crag would put me off the notion. That stretch of Derwent Water backed by these mountains...If it was good enough for Ruskin, it's good enough for me!'

Driving back over the stone humpback bridge at Grange, he saw their village nestling snugly in the valley with the crags towering above it. To him it was beautiful, but perhaps it had seemed like a prison to Beth. He was sure that this change had only occurred in her recently. She had enjoyed living here, or so she said, but now that she had reached her fifties, did she feel she was trapped? He knew growing old was a severe worry to her. He had pointed out to her that you could count on longevity here, but she hadn't been impressed. And anyway, could he use that argument now?

In the past she had often talked of London and how she had 'escaped' there from Maidstone, but in these days of travel, it wasn't totally inaccessible, surely, and there were cities nearer to them than London. Cities were for the young. Perhaps this current trip would make her realize that.

But the pleasant day he had spent hadn't stopped him worrying about his condition, which would soon be settled by his visit to the hospital. He began to think of the people it would affect. Beth, Laurel and Nick. And Mary? Well, it would be comforting to tell her, he had to admit to himself. She was a sensible, cheerful soul, and she was interested in his welfare. He had shirked confiding in her on his last visit. He would certainly do it tonight.

He arrived at her door, holding fast to his intention. She greeted him warmly, leading him through the garden room to the sitting room, where she had a fire blazing in the hearth.

When they were seated on the sofa, she turned to him. 'I'm glad you dropped in tonight, Sam. I had been thinking of you. Are you able to stay tonight?'

She looked very fetching, he thought, her hair glowing gold in the firelight, and there was a pleasant scent from her as if she had just showered – a clean, pleasant smell of rose.

'Yes, if you would like me to. I've got something to tell you, Mary.'

'Oh!' She gave him a searching look. 'Well, let's have a drink first.'

He watched her rump move in its silk sheath as she disappeared through the door. Beth had not put on weight with the menopause. Most women did. He could remember Mary Cass as a young girl in the village. She had been a good runner. At the school sports days he had admired how she ran, head up, knees up, not like the usual way of women, who only seemed to run from the knees. She was back in no time with two glasses of wine.

'I couldn't carry the bottle, but there's more where that came from.'

'Thank you.' He took a sip. 'Ah, good! Mary...'

'Yes?'

'I've been worried recently...'

'About us?'

'No. It's about me. You said I looked off-colour – well, there's a reason for that. I've recently had...symptoms, which made me see the doctor. I've been going through a series of tests...'

She put a hand over his. 'Oh, Sam! You should have confided in me.'

'There's no point in two of us worrying. There is the possibility of bad results...'

'Sam! Not...?'

The unspoken word, he thought. 'I thought I should warn you.'

'It would have been better if you had waited for the results.'

'Perhaps. But I didn't want to spring it on you, if the news were bad.'

She didn't speak for what seemed a long time, then she turned to face him. 'I'm turning it over in my mind, Sam. If it's what I think you're referring to, you do see it would make a difference in our relationship. I'm not good at looking after invalids. And if you were living with me, as an invalid, what would Rachel and William think? They wouldn't want to come here. It's not what I had envisaged. I thought of them taking to you, and enjoying visiting us, but now...'

Looking at her worried face, he saw it had been a mistake to confide in her. He had been looking for a mother, someone who would face the results with him, comfort him, but how could he expect Mary Cass to do that?

'You do see it alters everything, Sam, don't you?'

'Yes, if the results are bad. But I'm hoping...'

'How many tests have you had?'

'About three. This one will finally show whether I have cancer or not...I won't go into details, but sometimes they leave things to sort themselves out, or operate, or whatever...without Beth, what I need is someone like you to comfort me, help me to look on the bright side...'

'This is terrible, Sam. Of course I'm sorry for you, but I'm afraid I can't see us living together. I'm no good at illness, I think. With Bob it was a clean, sudden death, a terrible shock at the time, but once you get over the shock, you feel grateful that there wasn't a long illness. I'm a hopeless nurse.'

He took another sip of wine, then emptied

184

the glass. 'Well, I've got it out. It gives you time to think about what life might be with me, and I can see that you wouldn't want me here, even though nothing has happened yet. I'm living on a knife edge.' Beth could do it, he thought. She was always at her best in a crisis, always good at putting herself in someone else's place. Her trouble was that she couldn't deal with her own life, or why would she have left him now? 'You've made yourself quite clear, Mary. I think we can say our affair is over, before it's properly begun.'

'I'm so sorry, Sam, but I simply couldn't land myself in such a situation with you. I had to think long and hard about opening my door to you, because I have a lovely life here, independent, able to do what I like, have anyone here if I like...'

He held up his hand. 'Don't say any more. Apart from this, neither of us were ready for an affair. At our ages we think too much, we don't plunge into things the way the young do...I'll go now.' He got to his feet. 'Thanks for the wine, thanks for being so frank.'

'Stay and talk, Sam?'

'No, thank you, I can think better in my own house.'

'Will you let me know the results? I'm really very interested, you know that, and I'm very fond of you.'

'Thanks, Mary. I've enjoyed coming here.'

'Please don't stop. You have to keep coming to see the garden, at least.'

He didn't reply. 'Look after your polyanthus' might be a good exit line. Have you gone mad? he wondered, getting into his car.

When he got home he sat in the lounge, thinking, not sure what to do. Should he phone Beth? See what her reaction would be? No, there was nothing worse than bad news over the telephone. But you haven't had any news, he told himself. The waiting is getting to you. Your first decision was the right one, not to tell Beth until you knew. Unlike Mary, she might feel that he was bribing her to come back. No, he would wait.

He picked up the *Radio Times*. He'd find a good programme and concentrate on that until it was time to go to bed. And perhaps she would phone him. He realized he hadn't eaten. He went to the refrigerator and found in it a packet of pork sausages and some eggs. That was it. Toad-in-the-hole. It had been Laurel's favourite. Now it would be caviar. Good for Laurel, he thought.

Eleven

Beth had had a talk with Laurel one night before Jake came home. 'I've enjoyed myself in New York, Laurel,' she said. 'And you and Jake have been very good to me. I hope I haven't been too troublesome.'

'What nonsense, Mum! You know we've liked having you.'

'Despite my behaviour at Sag Harbour?'

'I don't know what you're talking about ...Yes, I do. Jake has had a talk with me. Said I had no right to be critical of my mother. I'm sorry if I offended you.'

'Jake's right. But I see now where I've gone wrong. You have a picture in your mind of how a mother must behave, and I had one about a daughter.'

'That's what Jake says. Get realistic, he says. Of course, he had the benefit of an unsettled childhood.'

'I had thought a settled childhood was more of a benefit.'

'No, it isn't, I've discovered. Jake thinks I'm too hard on you. He admires you greatly. "Classy", he says.'

I know what's been worrying her, Beth thought. She thinks I shouldn't have left Sam.

'I'd like to take you out to lunch, Laurel, as a perfect mother should, and we can have a proper chat. Jake will be in soon,' she said.

'OK. But you know it's because I love you that I get concerned about you.'

'Same here, and it's been like that ever since you were born. You'll know all about that when you have children of your own.'

'Jake and I have agreed to wait, to see how the marriage goes.'

'What a careful pair you are! Is that the modern way of thinking?'

'I don't know. But it's how *we* think.'

Jake burst in, full of life. 'You two having a gossip? Good. What about a drink?' He crossed to the table where the bottles stood. 'We'll miss you when you go, Beth. We've enjoyed having you.'

Looking at him, in all his handsomeness, she thought maybe Laurel was right. Any girl would fall for him, and if he took after his mother then he wasn't a good bet. She and Sam had never thought twice about having babies, it was what they both wanted. But then again, was that just the way it was when they were young? How the world has changed, she thought. She seemed to remember her own mother, who had been a bit of a complainer in her nursing home in Kent, saying the same thing.

Laurel had given Beth the number of the bus she had to take to Murray Hill, where the restaurant was situated near the gallery. She had suggested that Beth should come to the gallery, but she had declined. She didn't want to meet Joe again, was content to have known him briefly, and happy that they had made friends. She'd write to Maddy before she left New York, a friendly letter, wishing her good luck, and saying how glad she was to have met her, and how sorry she was that they hadn't met again.

She allowed plenty of time and was shown to a table by the window when she mentioned Laurel's name. She had time to admire the restaurant, since she was early for their lunch. It seemed quietly elegant, with quiet pictures on the walls, prints of the impressionists, she noticed with pleasure. The conversation in the background was hushed, as if the diners, mostly women, had been advised to lower their voices. Very different from Hilde Barube's party, she thought. Despite her demeanour, there had been a *louche*, voyeuristic air about Hilde Barube, as if she had arranged the party for her own benefit. Beth had sat meekly at the woman's side, like a child, rather than a woman of fifty-five, which was all the more surprising since in her own background she knew she was regarded as being smart, from the south, and had liked to give that impression. She had always made trips to London on her own, meeting school friends, taking tea in Fortnum and Mason, shopping in Harrods, and going to galleries. You, my girl, are having to make a complete reappraisal of yourself.

She looked up and saw her daughter making her way through the tables to where she was sitting, and saw how Laurel fitted into this environment, had made it her own. It was more than fate that she had gone to Hong Kong and met Jake there. She was suited to this environment and had welcomed it when it presented itself to her.

'Well, Mum, you got here before me. Good for you!' Laurel kissed her mother's cheek.

'I have travelled on buses before, Laurel.'

'You're touchy this morning.' She was now sitting across from Beth, and she smiled.

'Sorry. Perhaps I object to being treated as someone who doesn't know her way about.'

To her surprise, Laurel put her hand over hers. 'Oh, Mum,' she said. 'You're missing Dad, aren't you?'

'Is that what you think?'

'Don't let us quarrel. This is our last time to have a talk before you go off to Nick's. You'll probably do better there. He's always been your favourite.'

'That's been your belief since you were a little girl. We love you both equally.'

'I hope you're prepared to face up to the fact that he's gay. He wanted me to tell you, but I said he had to do his own dirty work.'

'I think he's got every intention of telling mc when I meet him. He's putting me up at a hotel to begin with.'

'Poor Nick. He's still doubtful of your reaction.'

'It's his father he ought to worry about. He's the one who finds it difficult, but I accepted the possibility long ago.'

'You'll like Chris. He's got a good sense of humour. And he's a good cook. Nick's a lazy devil. He lets Chris do it all. How long are you staying there?'

'Two weeks, I hope. I said to your father, six weeks, allowing two weeks with each of you and the remainder for travelling.'

'What was the urge, Mum? Was it to see us both, where, and how, we lived?'

'Perhaps. And to have a talk with you.'

'What was this talk to be about?'

She met her daughter's eyes, and thought, they're Sam's eyes. They pin you down by their honesty. 'You'll find this hard to believe, Laurel...' But the waiter had interrupted and presented them both with menus.

'Anything you choose here, you'll like, Mum. It's women's fare, easy on the digestion.'

'You choose, Laurel.'

'Their fish pie is delicious.' Laurel nodded to the waiter, pointing. 'And a bottle of Chablis please, Guy.'

'We'll never drink a whole bottle, Laurel!'

'You'll be surprised what New York does to you. Anyhow, we can leave what we don't drink.' When the waiter went away she asked, 'What was the talk to be about, Mum?'

'I wanted to confide in you. You'll find this hard to believe, but when we were in Gran Canaria, I thought, well, I'm with Sam for the rest of my life. And it frightened me.' She had said it.

'But you couldn't be with a nicer person for the rest of your life! And why not the person you've spent most of your life with? You and Dad were marvellous to me about that fire. You never once said I told you so, and Dad appreciated how upset I was about Dave.'

'Yes, I know, Laurel. If I did say anything about it, I felt it wouldn't sound sincere, since I'd been opposed to you going to London in the first place. Children believe that their parents are opposing them when what they're doing is trying to save them from hurt.'

'You didn't trust me. And, believe it or not, that's what I've been trying to do with you here! Protect you. I felt you were in a reckless mood, and I was afraid for Dad's sake, that you'd get tangled up with someone like Joe or Blaise Carey, because you were missing Dad, and you'd regret it later.'

'How do you know I'm missing Dad?'

'It's written all over you, and you constantly refer to him. "Dad would like this" or, "I wonder what Dad would say if he saw..." You're so used to being with him that you can't enjoy yourself on your own. You thought you could when you left home, but I bet you've found out you can't.'

'The oracle speaks.'

'Don't be cheeky.' She smiled at Beth to show she didn't mind a spat. 'Nick would tell you the same as I'm telling you. We've both chosen our lives, and I think we're both clear-sighted about it. Nick worries that Chris might leave him, and knowing Jake's background, I'm prepared for him having affairs.'

'Jake would never do that.'

'You don't know Jake.'

They were on their second glass of Chablis. Beth had loved the delicate fish pie with its equally delicate sauce. They had exchanged many confidences, except one.

'There is one thing I haven't told you, Laurel,' Beth said. 'Sam had started an affair with Mary Cass.'

'Dad? No!' Her eyes were round. 'Was that why you took off?'

'No, he only told me when I told him I wanted a trial separation. I felt very jealous, but I had burned my boats, so to speak. But he gave me a good excuse, although when I told him about wanting to go, he thought I might be depressed.'

'Do you think you were?'

'I think I must have been, because the whole idea seems rather ridiculous to me now.'

'That proves it. Was Dad serious about Mary Cass, or was it a slip-up?'

'To be fair to him, I think it was a slip-up. I realize that now, but at the time…Well, you can imagine.'

'Maybe *he* was depressed.'

'Dad never gets depressed.'

'You don't know that. Slip-ups are often caused by depression.'

'I think you've been influenced by Lia. She offered me her therapist.'

'Oh, Lia! Shall you still go on to Hong Kong?'

'Yes, I'm going to have my six weeks' holiday. My ticket is booked. The bonus is seeing you and Nicholas.'

'How like you that is! You wouldn't think of going back now?'

'No, I have to stick to my guns.'

'That's my mum!' She was smiling. 'You're very young for your age, which makes it easy for us to talk to each other. I think I understand you. Do you understand me?'

'You're harder than me, but I think that's because of the times we live in. You've adapted to them.'

'Have to. It's funny to hear you say that I'm harder than you, but most children are harder than their parents – realistic, whereas the children thought that their parents were the hard ones. We're arguing from different perspectives. Time marches on, and we don't take that into account.'

'This doesn't sound like my Laurel talking. Where did you learn all this?'

'Life. Jake. I'm a quick learner. I bet the next scenario will be when my marriage is on the rocks, and I come back to you for advice.'

'I hope that doesn't happen, but if it does, I hope I'll be able to give it. Tell me, Laurel, this is the thing that mothers always long to ask their daughters. Do you think I'm attractive?'

'Why do you ask?'

'I seem to have lost myself. I always thought I was, and I think I actually felt I was *buried* in the Lakes, unappreciated, miles away from London, where I should have been.'

'Shall I tell you that I used to be madly

jealous of you?'

'Shall I tell you that, deep down, I think I was madly jealous of you going to London?'

'That's why I went there. To become soignée, like you. Then I found that I could only be my own person.' She lifted the bottle. 'Let's have another glass of Chablis, in case we become too sentimental. I shan't be able to see Joe's pictures straight when I get back, but what the hell!'

They drank to each other, smiling over their glasses.

Twelve

Nicholas was waiting for her at the arrivals gate of Hong King airport and whisked her away in his car. He seemed anxious, and apart from asking her if she'd had a good flight, and how Sam and Laurel were, didn't say very much.

In a way she was glad, because it meant she was free to form an impression of Hong Kong – to look at the streets with the rickshaws darting between cars. Apart from the rickshaws, it seemed very much like the streets of New York. Hong Kong had the same air of bustle, with people hurrying along, looking ahead, intent on some goal they had in their minds. Only the cultural mix was different. This living in large cities, she decided, didn't appeal to her now – you had to be young, with a goal, to stand the constant noise and pressure.

Life was leisurely at home, peaceful. She thought of the roads she drove on through the fells, the usual emptiness, the calming landscape around her. Only occasionally did she have to pull over when the country bus came along. She hadn't appreciated the quietness at the time but now, away from it, she did. It was that peace that brought the townies and the walkers, who swarmed over the fells and filled the pubs. Certainly the poets like Wordsworth and Coleridge who had come to the Lakes and stayed, had appreciated it, and had first coined that overused phrase, 'communion with nature'.

'Do you like living in cities?' she asked Nicholas.

'Love them,' he said. 'I sometimes leave the car in the garage and walk to work, just for the buzz.'

'In New York,' she said, 'I often saw business-girls in suits and wearing trainers, walking briskly in the streets. I asked Laurel if it was their lunch they carried in those briefcases, and she said possibly, but certainly their high-heeled shoes for the office.'

'That could be true, but I often think of the peace and calm when I went climbing with Dad, and when we got to the top, sitting, not speaking, with those wonderful views spread around us, and often a heron sailing above. I'll retire here, I would say to myself, I couldn't leave this.'

'But you and Laurel ran away to the cities.'

'That's natural for the young. But one keeps the picture in one's mind, and resolves to go back sometime.'

It became right for you, she thought, you didn't realize that you were growing into it. Don't you remember driving up from Manchester or London, and how the first sight of the hills when you passed Preston gave you a feeling of coming home? She caught sight of some old faces amongst the crowds, and thought how incongruous they were. Were they the parents of younger children who had brought them from the Territories with the promise of a good life? Now they were like flowers in unsuitable soil, wilted. That could apply to her, she thought, only you have deserted your soil, and Sam.

'It's natural.' Nicholas, like her, was pursuing his own train of thought. 'You begin to feel buried. But you liked it, didn't you?' He spoke with his eyes on the traffic.

'Yes, I did. I realize that now that I've left it.'

'Only temporarily, Mother,' he said.

'I hope so.' She felt him give her a quick glance.

The hotel he took her to on Kowloon Harbour seemed luxurious, with the same impression of space that she had felt in Laurel's flat in New York. Was it because their lives were so cramped that they needed room, or was it that in newer cities there was more room to build in? London was old, cramped. When they were seated in the lounge and Nicholas had ordered drinks, she looked around and said, 'This is far too luxurious for me, Nicholas.'

A young Asian girl in a strapless dress, the skirt split up to the thigh, served their drinks. Her curved mouth was delicious, her ebony hair swung as she bent over the table to serve them. Beth noticed that Nicholas seemed quite unaffected as he thanked her.

'It's quite typical of Hong Kong,' he said. He didn't watch the girl going away. She had often seen the appreciative glances of men in a similar situation. 'Our apartment is near. I thought it would give us a chance to talk.'

She made up her mind. 'Is it about you being gay?'

His eyes met hers. 'Laurel would tell you. Somehow I found it too difficult to tell you and Dad. You're so backward up there. It's a different world.' That's contradicting what you've just said, she thought, and she felt hurt.

'I always thought we were quite up-to-date. But now that I've had experience of living in cities, I realize you could call it a backwater. I knew that, of course, and felt it when I first married, about your age. I was comparing it then with London. You could say I was bad at adapting.'

'We can put you up, Mother,' he said, leaning forward, as if what she was saying was of no account. 'I wanted to have a talk with you first. Chris would like to meet you. Laurel liked him.'

'I'm sure I shall. I'm quite prepared to meet him, and stay with you if you have room for me. It would be utterly ridiculous if I were in this hotel.' As she spoke, she wondered if she was telling the truth. The situation could be awkward.

'Chris and Laurel got on well together.' His face broadened in a reflective smile.

'Did you think he and I wouldn't?'

'Well, I remembered you being so critical of Laurel, when she was in London, that I was doubtful.'

'You might have given me the benefit of the doubt.'

'Chris isn't going to be critical of *you*.'

'Well, I hope not. I'll tell you what you should do. Go over to that desk and cancel my room, and then I'll come back with you to your flat.'

'No, that's not a good idea. You have a good rest here tonight after your flight, and that will give Chris time to plan a welcome dinner and get your room ready for you.'

'He sounds like the head cook and bottle-washer.'

'You're right. That's what he is. Oh, I'm

glad that you're coming to stay with us.'

'Dad and I don't live in the Middle Ages, Nicholas.'

'But you both care for your status in the town.'

'Staying with you and Chris shouldn't alter that. If it does, it wasn't worth having. And Nicholas, I want to have a talk with you, about Dad and me.' She made up her mind. 'Well, I came to a crossroads in my life, in Gran Canaria of all places. I had been ill before we went. Everything seemed flat. I suddenly realized I wasn't looking forward to our retirement together. I felt my life was coming to an end too soon. So I told him, and said I'd go away for a time and visit you and Laurel, and straighten myself out.'

'Poor Dad would be floored,' he said. 'I always thought you and he were admirably suited, when I thought about it at all. Children don't give much thought to their parents' happiness. They're too absorbed in finding out about themselves.'

'He wasn't exactly floored. He told me he had started an affair with Mary Cass.'

'Never!' He looked astonished. 'But she's

nothing like you!'

'That's probably the point. I don't think I'm easy to live with, Nicholas. I was so busy wondering about myself that I never gave any thought to how Dad felt about our marriage. It was a status quo. Something you stick to, or on occasion go away from, knowing that it would be there when you came back.'

'But, Mary Cass! She's dull, she hasn't got your personality, or looks!'

'Thanks for those few kind words. Maybe it was a mid-life crisis. The affair seemed to happen when I was with Gran – if you remember, I went to Maidstone to look after her. But Mary Cass is easy. As you know, I'm not.'

'You were all right with me. You didn't kick up a fuss about me dropping out.'

'I think fathers feel that more acutely. Besides, you were always my favourite.' She smiled at him. The first-born. 'But as you said, I was hard on Laurel, not understanding. That's typical of mothers, I think. I wonder if it is because we envy our daughters having a better time than we had, especially in this day and age. We can't compare ourselves with our sons, so there's no envy there.'

'Dad was disappointed with me leaving university.'

'Well, pride comes into it there. They like to boast about how well their sons are doing.'

'And was it a further blow to him about me and Chris?'

'Well, think of his upbringing. I played the part of being worldly-wise, and he had to accept my viewpoint. It's a competition with other fathers in his case. It boosts their ego. And he fancied the idea of someone coming into the shop and enquiring about you, and he would be able to say, "He's turning out to be a very good batter, or swimmer, or he's scooping up all the prizes. Not like his father, ha ha. Only a shopkeeper."'

'Well, I did climb.'

'But so did he. It had to be something intellectual.'

'I wonder if he was disappointed that I didn't come into the shop with him. Third generation.'

'Oh, no, he always thought you were too good for that.'

'Of course, I knew that. That's why I dropped out, I felt I was letting him down. Mother, perhaps if you like Chris, you could ask him to come home with me sometime and meet Dad. He's curious about the Lakes, envies me, he's into nature in a big way, reads poetry. We have a tame blackbird that knocks on our window every morning. Chris feeds it. His home was London.'

'Yes, you know I've always encouraged you to bring friends to the house. But, we'll have to see how Dad does...' She looked at him and wanted to weep. He had always been sympathetic.

He put his hand over hers and said, 'It's going to be all right, Mother.' The pain was still in her heart. She wiped her eyes with her handkerchief. 'I got this from Mrs Cochrane. It's come in useful. A plastic tube with three in it.'

'Good for old Mrs Cochrane.'

'Tell me about Chris. Has he parents?' She concentrated on this son of hers whom she loved.

'A mother. She's typically Sloane Square. I think she believes it's a feather in her cap, having a son who's gay. And she's not the type that's into grandchildren.' Beth could see her, a sharp, thin woman of a certain age, shopping in Harrods, playing bridge in the afternoon, going to see all the gallery exhibitions, Wimbledon, Henley, because all her friends did and it was the thing to do. How would she fare, she wondered, smiling, if she attended a fell race?

'What are you smiling at, Mother?' he asked, giving her a quick glance.

'I was thinking of her watching a hundred young men in shorts and singlets with their water bottles, running up and down crags, just for pleasure, and her astonishment.'

'Not a patch on Ascot, eh?'

'Or going to see the sheep-shearing?'

'Now that might appeal more. She could buy a sheepskin rug in our shop, I'm sure Dad keeps them. He was always talking about diversifying, and she could boast she had bought it in the Lakes.'

'Like china from the Harrods sale. We mustn't laugh. So you're not cancelling my room here?'

'No, I think this is better. We've had a jolly good talk, broken the ice. I had arranged that dinner should be brought up to your room, but change that if you wish, and then you can shower and pop into bed.'

'Before that, I'm going to phone Dad and Laurel, and tell them that I've arrived.'

'And he wasn't badly upset about me?' His eyes were anxious.

'He didn't say. Perhaps he talked it over with Mary. He's like the men who he calls his friends – middle-class, middle-aged, prejudiced. I think his school was to blame, but Dad's amenable, takes knocks, doesn't go on about them.'

'I can't believe that he started an affair with Mary Cass! Of all people, fat, good-natured, but not at all like you.'

'A change is a good thing. After all, that's what I'm doing.'

'Do you miss him?'

'I do. I see now all the good points of having a man around to squire you.'

'More than that, I hope?' His eyes were grown-up eyes.

She didn't reply. 'Supposing you go and get the key to my room, Nicholas. I must phone him and tell him that I've arrived. And Laurel too.'

She kissed him goodbye outside her room and patted his shoulder. 'Don't worry,' she said, and promised to be ready in the morning to be picked up.

She thought she would sit and think for a bit. Nicholas had suggested that Sam had had a mid-life crisis. That seemed to be feasible. He was as entitled to one as she was. She lifted the telephone and dialled their own house number. 'Sam?' she asked when she heard his voice, a good-tempered voice.

'Beth! I've been waiting for you to ring. Did you have a good flight?'

'Yes, thank you.' Her tone, she knew, was dismissive, as befitted someone who was accustomed to flying. 'Nicholas met me. He has ensconced me in a lovely hotel on Kowloon Harbour where I can watch the boats, and digest the fact that I'm to meet his partner, Chris, tomorrow, and have dinner with them, which Chris will cook. I'm to stay at their flat.'

'You're going?'

'Certainly.'

'Beth...' She heard the hesitation in his voice. 'I've got something to tell you.'

Had Mary ditched him? 'Yes?'

'I haven't been well for some time, and I went to see Alan Barclay. He arranged an appointment with an urologist, and he put me through some tests...'

'And?' Her heart had made a leap into her throat. 'And?' she said again, trying to speak clearly. 'What was the result, Sam?'

'He suspects cancer. Prostate cancer.'

She couldn't speak for a moment. She cleared her throat. 'Cancer?' she repeated. 'So what do they do now?'

'I've been to hospital for a biopsy. I'm at home waiting for the results. I didn't want to ring you. But Alan said I should.'

'I should never have forgiven you if you had kept this secret from me. Besides, Nicholas has to be told. And Laurel.'

'It's probably a fuss about nothing.'

'I hope it is. Try not to worry. I'll come right away. I'll ask Nicholas to book a return flight for me. That way, I'll be home in time for the results.'

'Don't do that. Have your time with Nick.'

'No, I'm coming home. I'll let you know the time of my plane's arrival. Will you meet me at Manchester? Are you able to do that?'

'Of course. I feel fine. I'll be there.'

'I'll ring you when I get my ticket. Try not to worry.'

'I'm not worrying...now.' He felt he should say more, but was too overcome with happiness at the thought of seeing her that he was speechless.

'See you soon, Sam. Goodbye. I love you.'

'Me too,' he said, like a schoolboy, and hung up the phone.

Beth dialled Laurel's number immediately. She heard her voice with its faint American accent, its upward inflection.

'Mum? You've arrived safely?'

'Yes, good flight.'

'Anyone in the next seat to you?'

'An elderly lady who talked non-stop about her grandchildren. I'd rather have had Reggie Connor.'

'You're becoming quite a flirt in your

old age.'

She disregarded the remark. 'Laurel, I phoned Dad, and he's waiting for the results of a biopsy. He became ill after I left...' She stopped to think. 'No, I expect he had the symptoms when I was at home and he didn't tell me...'

'What's the biopsy for?'

'Cancer. Prostate cancer.' It helped to say the word. 'He is expecting the results pretty soon. I'm setting off for home straight away.'

'Even if the result is good?'

She was surprised at Laurel's remark. Was she testing her? She dismissed that. Laurel hadn't been married a long time like her. One shared the good and the bad.

'Poor Dad! All alone.'

'I'll let you know,' said Beth.

'OK. But I'll phone him, cheer him up.'

'He seems to be taking it very well.'

'That was for your benefit. Have you met Chris Barbour yet?'

'No, I'm in a hotel for the night. It was Nicholas's idea.'

'He worried about you meeting Chris.'

'He shouldn't have. I'm going to hang up,

Laurel. Love to you and Jake.'

'Same to you. Try to look on the bright side, Mum.'

'It was sensible of Dad to go to the doctor. You know what he's like. Hasn't any time for them, even Alan.'

'It proves he was worried.'

'Yes. Goodbye, Laurel.' She hung up.

When she had eaten her dinner, which, as Nicholas had said, was light, and drank the glass of wine the waiter had poured out for her, she undressed, had a shower and got into bed. This was the second blow Sam had dealt her – first Mary and then about this test. Waiting for the results must be agony for him. He had always been impatient. Poor Sam, on his own, waiting...Hot tears welled up in her eyes. I've deserted him, she thought, just when he needed me. Fate had been against her. But at least it had proved to her that she didn't want to leave him.

She pictured him in their house, wandering about, going into the garden for comfort, or his shed, or there was that seat at the beck, then coming back again, slumping in his chair opposite the television set. They had joked that if they put an umbrella over him, he would be quite content there, wouldn't need a house. He didn't even have a cat or dog to comfort him. They had decided, or she had decided, that pets would only prevent them from going off on sudden holidays when the fancy took them. Prince, his labrador, had conveniently, it seemed then, got run over, which removed him from the house, and Daisy, the cat, had come to the end of her useful life, which consisted of climbing up on convenient knees or beds for mutual comfort, usually hers. Then poor Daisy had got rheumatism and couldn't jump up on to her knee, or the bed, and had lain in her own bed by the Aga, smelling dreadfully, until Sam took the matter into his own hands, taking her to the vet to be put down, and rendering them both petless. It had been sad, washing the bowls labelled DOG and CAT, and putting them away, perhaps for future use, they said, although they both knew that Prince and Daisy wouldn't be replaced.

She wept for a long time, then got up and poured some wine from the bottle into a glass and took it back to bed with her.

To her surprise she slept well, but wakened with thoughts of Sam on her mind. You've been selfish, she told herself, it was what *you* wanted that mattered, you took off without considering what he would think, but then again...She remembered Mary Cass.

She crossed to the wide window and saw some men standing on the pavement with their backs to her, gazing towards the harbour. But they were not merely gazing. Their arms and legs were moving in a stylistic manner. Each man seemed to be wrapped in his own world. Shadow-boxing? Was there a metaphor there?

Nicholas hadn't told her about this peculiar practice when he was telling her about the sights of Hong Kong. If I were younger, she thought, I should have gone down and investigated, but she reflected that one lost one's courage and one's curiosity as one grew older. When she had dressed, she tried out some of the poses she had watched, growling fearfully at herself in the mirror. Complete exercise, she thought, face included. And one didn't behave like that if one's husband were around.

What if that state, of being husbandless, were permanent? She hadn't used her brain. Although she had been able to imagine leaving him for a time, she had never thought of how she would feel if she were alone permanently. Badly thought-out. And now his news...

The telephone rang in her room and she thought it might be Sam. Her heart was beating loudly as she lifted the receiver. It was the man at reception.

'Mr Crome is waiting for you in the lobby, Mrs Crome.'

'Thank you. I'll be down right away.'

Nicholas got up from a seat when she appeared. 'Here I am. Did you sleep well, Mother?'

'Yes, I woke early and watched some men striking strange poses from my window. Nothing I would see at home.'

'Tai Chi. If you go into any of the parks you see it being practised. Chris and I often try it, going to the nearby park and joining the old men. We enjoy making fearful faces at each other.' His smile was broad.

'Do you?' she asked innocently.

In the car, when he had stowed away her cases, he said, 'I hope we can make you as comfortable as at the hotel. You'll have the apartment to yourself in the daytime, so you can do what you like.'

'I might go to your park and join the old men.' I'm talking like this because I'm nervous, she thought.

'Did you phone Dad and Laurel?' he asked her.

'Yes, and I've got some news for you. I hope it's not a shock. Dad has had a biopsy. They thought it might be cancer of the prostate.'

He said, after a pause, 'What's the result?'

'He hasn't had it yet, but regardless of that, Nicholas, I don't think I'll stay with you for long. I should like to be at home with him.'

'You're quite right. He must be worried, and he would want your company.'

'That's what I thought, and I've told Dad I'll fly home as soon as possible. I thought you might phone and book a return ticket for me, then I'll let him know when to expect me.'

'Yes, I'll do that. Did you tell Laurel?'

'Yes, I did.'

'We'll just have to hope that his news, when it comes, is good.'

'Yes.'

He put a hand over hers. 'Don't worry, Mother. We'll get you a ticket as soon as we can. Then you can phone Dad from our flat.'

'Yes, of course. I'll go and see Alan Barclay when I go home, and have a chat with him.'

'He'll put you in the picture. Here we are!' He had pulled into a parking space in front of an imposing block of flats. 'This is where we live. It's too busy here,' he said, after a quick look round. 'I think I'll drive into the underground car park.' There, he helped her out then took her cases out of the boot, and directed her towards an elevator. On the way up, he said, 'Try not to worry, Mother. The news will probably be good.' She smiled and nodded, trying to keep the remnants of the smile in place.

He unlocked the door of the flat and

ushered her in, calling at the same time, 'We're here, Chris!'

A man – she could hardly call him a boy, but then Nick was twenty-five – appeared from one of the doors leading off the hall. He came towards Beth, smiling, hand outstretched. 'Well, hello, Mrs Crome. This son of yours has told me so much about you.'

'I hope it was good.' She liked the look of him. He seemed what she called reliable – tall, bald, with a humorous mouth, and with the air of someone who dealt with the public.

'Come into the lounge. We'll have coffee, if that suits you.'

'Oh, yes.' It was a large room, unmistakably a men's room. There were no flowers, surfaces were cluttered with magazines, cameras – for observing Tai Chi, she thought, and although she disliked clutter, she thought it looked comfortable, cosy even. There was a piano in a corner.

'Sit down where you like, Mother,' Nicholas said. She chose an armchair near the window. It didn't look on to the harbour, as the hotel had done, but she could see there was a pleasant space of green with plenty of trees on the other side of the road, probably the park Nick had referred to. The road between it and the flats were busy with cars. 'I'll put your cases in your room.'

'And I'll bring in the coffee,' Chris Barbour said. 'See how you're going to be waited on!' His smile was charming and assured, as if he knew that she was ill at ease.

'My mother has had worrying news about my father,' Nick said to Chris when he came back with a tray. 'He's had tests done for prostate cancer, but they haven't got the result yet.'

'Oh, bad luck!' Chris said. 'Yes, you must be worried, Mrs Crome. I believe in the majority of cases it proves to be nothing to be worried about.'

'I hope you're right,' she said, feeling incredibly heartened.

Was he a doctor? Nicholas hadn't told her his occupation.

'So I may not be a visitor for long,' she said, 'but I felt since I'd come to see Nick, I'd be better here.'

'I'm sure that's what Nick would like,' he said, glancing at him.

'Sure! So how about pouring the coffee, bonzo? While you're doing that, I'll go and see if I can book the plane.'

'Did you know you have a bossy son?' Chris said, glancing at Beth. I like this man, she thought, trying to see him as a partner of her son's.

'I think that's what Nick would accuse *me* of,' she said. 'And Laurel. Children always think they're being bossed about by their parents. So as soon as they can, they start being bossy themselves.'

Nicholas came back, smiling. 'No trouble, Mother. I've got a ticket for you for tomorrow morning.'

She felt glad of their company as they chatted and drank their coffee. The young men were at ease, which made her feel the same.

When Chris was in the kitchen, Nicholas said to Beth, 'Try not to worry, Mother. We'll go out in the afternoon and see Hong Kong, and then come back here for dinner and you can phone Dad whenever you like.

The time will soon pass. And you're better here with us than being on your own in the hotel.'

'That's what I thought,' she said.

They seemed determined to amuse her as they all chatted together. And she grew to like Chris. They're very well suited, she thought, remembering that was what she had thought when Laurel had brought Jake home. But then Laurel had always been able to look after herself, while Nicholas had needed support, had been less sure of himself, and everything, even his leaving university, was typical of his unsureness. He had decided to read maths and physics at first, and then, compared with his fellow students, thought he wasn't good enough. 'You should see the work some of them produce,' he had told Sam.

'That's Nicholas,' she had said later, when he had gone. 'Never sure of himself, nothing will convince him.' Perhaps he had needed someone like Chris to look up to.

She asked Chris what he did, and he said he worked in a bank, that Hong Kong was the place where they made the money.

He exploded with laughter as he said this and looked across at Nicholas, who joined in.

'This fool said that when he was a child some friend of his parents had said, in his presence, that one could make a lot of money in Hong Kong, and he had taken that literally.'

Chris explained. 'I imagined Hong Kong as a place where there were big machines turning out banknotes all the time, Mrs Crome, and so when I got the chance to come to the Hong Kong branch of the bank, I jumped at it. But I've still to find those machines!'

When Beth went with Nicholas to see her room, he showed her round the flat – the kitchen, where Chris was busy, wearing a butcher's apron, and the gym which they had installed in one of the rooms. Her own room was functional, fully equipped like the hotel, and with lots of room in the cupboards for her clothes. She decided not to unpack until she heard from Sam. The three of them set out for lunch, stopping at Nathan Road so that she could see the shops. They had lunch in a smart restaurant, where she was introduced to dim sum, which she confessed she had never tasted. The noise inside, of music, English and Chinese voices and laughter was, she imagined, the atmosphere they both liked. They seemed animated, and several friends came up to their table to speak to them, who in turn were introduced to her, all exquisitely polite. She felt herself to be a favoured person in this milieu.

They got back to the flat about six o'clock after driving to see Victoria Peak and Aberdeen harbour. 'This is where Laurel and Jake met,' Nicholas told her. 'She called it a pick-up.'

When they got back, Chris disappeared into the kitchen, while she and Nicholas listened to his tapes. 'Chris plays the piano,' he said. 'It's his. We're into the music scene here, and go dancing quite a lot.' That made her wonder if they danced together, but the idea and then the picture were dismissed from her mind. She hadn't seen any outward signs of their relationship, as she had with Jake and Laurel. They insulted each other unequivocally, like two puppies snapping playfully at each other, she thought. She kept her mind firmly on the present, wishing Sam would call.

Chris came into the lounge. 'Dinner is ready. Shall we have a drink first?'

'I was hoping you would play for us, Chris,' Beth said. 'Nick's been telling me of your prowess.'

'After dinner?' he said. 'You may not like my playing. It's all jazz, a mixture of old and new.'

'He picks up tunes from the tapes,' Nicholas said, looking proud.

'Champion, the wonder horse!' Chris sang. 'Come along then, Mrs Crome. You need sustenance to put up with my playing.'

The flat seemed to be wired for sound, music flowed round them in the kitchen-dining room, filled in the spaces while Chris was busy at the stove, or while Nicholas cleared the plates, and formed a background to their chatter round the table. The meal was different from what she was in the habit of cooking at home, the ingredients were strange, with an abundance of fruit and vegetables that she didn't recognize. She was asked to comment on the wine Nicholas poured, as if she was a connoisseur. The atmosphere was merry, she felt like an honoured guest, and sometimes she saw the two men exchanging glances of appreciation at something she said. She felt that behind it was kindness, that they were endeavouring to cheer her, that they understood she would be waiting for Sam's phone call. When they left the table, they were all thoroughly at ease. She felt as if she had been accepted by them, and no doubt Nicholas felt she had accepted Chris, even approved of him.

After dinner, when they were having coffee, the telephone rang. Nicholas got up from his chair, saying, 'I wonder who this is?' They were sitting in the lounge, and when he came back Beth looked at him enquiringly. 'It's Dad, Mother! He wants to speak to you. Why don't you go into our room? You'll be more private there.'

She followed him into a bedroom where she sat down on one of the twin beds. She had a faint impression of men's belongings spread out on surfaces – ties, books, keys – and on the bed, which she hadn't sat on, there was a blue dressing gown which she recognized as belonging to Nicholas.

'The phone's there between the beds,' Nicholas said. 'I'll go and hang up the one in the hall.'

Apprehension made her hand tremble as she took the telephone from its cradle. 'Hello, Sam,' she said. 'How are you?'

'Fine. I thought I'd save you the bother of phoning me.' Her heart leapt. 'I had a chat with Nick and told him. I'm sorry to have alarmed you all when I've nothing to report.'

'I'm glad you phoned. Nick has booked for me to leave tomorrow morning.'

'Yes, he gave me the time of your arrival. I'll be there to meet you. Are you sure you want to do this, Beth? I'm spoiling your time with him.'

'No, you're not. I've seen him and met Chris. How do you feel?'

'Strangely enough, very well. I think it's having you and the family to share it with.'

'Who better than your own family?'

'I had a call from Laurel last night. She cheered me up no end. How are you getting on with Chris?'

'Very well. He's charming, has a good sense of humour, and I think he'll look after Nick very well. I'm happy about them, Sam. We'll talk about them when I get home. I'm looking forward to seeing you.' She didn't want to ask him about Mary. This was a family affair.

'Me too. Goodbye. Safe journey.'

'Thanks.'

They both raised expectant faces to her when she went into the lounge.

'No news yet. He told you, Nicholas,' she said.

'Yes. Any further details?'

'No. I think they won't keep him waiting long. He's bound to be a bit apprehensive. I think he's pleased I'm coming home.'

'I'm sure he is,' Chris said, and Nick nodded. 'I've to fly off to the islands to arrange some holiday packages. I'll see you on to your plane first.'

'So perhaps it's a good thing I'm going.'

'No, not at all, I should have been back

231

tomorrow evening in any case.'

'So I'm a short-term guest, Chris,' she said, smiling at him. 'I'm sorry I shan't have more of your dinners. Tonight's was delightful.'

'You must come back. Now that you've broken the ice.'

'Yes, that's right.' She smiled round at both of them. 'What about you playing, Chris? You promised me.'

'Certainly.'

He played old blues songs, mixed with definitely romantic ones, and pop – some of which, to her uneducated ears, were simply a cacophony of noise, then back again to the blues.

'That's a favourite one of Billie Holiday's, isn't it, Chris?' Nick asked, and got to his feet. 'Come on, Mother. May I have this dance?' He bowed to her.

She got up, laughing. 'This is a new experience for me. I don't think I've ever danced with you, Nick.'

'You don't know what you've missed.' He whirled her round and then steered her into the middle of the room. If this were Sam, she thought...You weren't supposed to have any feelings when you danced with your son, but this was a very sexy song.

'Very elegant,' Chris said to them, smiling from his seat at the piano. 'I envy you your partner, Nick.'

'If I could take your place there, I would.' Nick whirled her round when they reached him. 'What about some boogie-woogie?'

'You've got it.' He bent over his hands.

The sound seemed to lift her up and swing her round the room. It was exhilarating. She forgot she was dancing with Nick; it was like all the dances she'd ever had with Sam rolled into one. When he whirled her and again, she broke away from him and fell back on to the sofa. 'You forget your mum is an old lady now,' she said.

'I wouldn't think so,' Chris said from the piano. 'Anyhow, the pianist is going to stop for a thirst-quenching drink.'

They had a final drink 'to round off the evening', as Chris said.

Beth's spirits had flagged. Poor Sam, she thought. I shouldn't have left him, nor should I be enjoying myself like this.

'Are you tired, Mother?' Nicholas asked.

'A bit. I think I'll go to bed. What time do you leave, Chris?'

'Around eight.'

'Well, we'll leave goodbyes till then.' She got up.

Young company was tiring, she thought as she undressed in her room. She and Sam were the right age for each other. *If he's spared.* The words suddenly occurred to her. It was an expression they used in the north. She knew now that she wanted to share what was left of her life with him, not as a wanderer round the world, nor as a guest in her children's homes. To be happy, one had to know one's place.

She found herself weeping when she said goodbye to Nicholas at the airport.

'Sorry, Nick. I'm not usually like this. I should have liked to have more time with you, but you know I'm worried about Dad.'

'I'm sure it's going to be all right, Mother. And I'm so glad you visited us. Now that you've met Chris and like him, it's a great load off my mind.'

'I've enjoyed seeing you and Laurel settled in your homes with people you're happy with. My trip has been worthwhile.'

On the plane going home, Beth felt as if she had grown in some way by her decision to go off and visit the two children. They were both happy, and that was a good thing. And she would have their support if Sam's news was not good. I'm lucky, she said to herself.

There was a young man sitting beside her, and apart from exchanging a few words, she decided that she didn't need to speak. He probably wasn't interested in her in any case. She enjoyed the journey, letting her mind roam over her visits to New York and Hong Kong, but now she was going back to Sam. Her whole attitude had changed. He needed her. She was no longer needed by her family, but she might need *them*. Just as Sam might. What about Mary Cass? she wondered. But she seemed unimportant now, an intruder who would fade away when she got back home.

Thirteen

Sam was at the arrivals gate waiting for her. Beth thought he looked pale and strained, and felt immediately guilty. She should have been with him when he needed her. He put his arms round her and kissed her, not speaking, and she said, looking up at him, 'It was almost worth while going away to have such a welcome.'

'I've missed you,' he said and, putting her cases in the trolley he had ready, he put his arm round her and together they walked to the car park.

'Any word yet?' She had to ask.

'Wait till we're in the car and I'll tell you,' he said, and they talked about the children until they reached it.

'Well?' she said when they were settled in the car. 'Have you heard?'

'Alan phoned them. It's a question now of waiting for the pathologist's report. Yea or nay.'

'Well, it's a good thing I'm back,' she said, and put her hand over his on the wheel. 'We can wait together.'

After a time she said, 'Have you told Mary Cass?'

'Yes, I told her that I was having the test done. She was sorry, of course, but...The affair's over, if it ever started.'

She felt a smile creep over her face and controlled it before she spoke. 'Well, that's all right then. But you've still got me.'

'Have I got you, Beth?' he asked.

'Of course. I haven't come back only because of what's happened – I missed you all the time. I should have come back in any case. There's no place for me away from you.' She patted his hand and then sat up straight and looked around. Not long now until they would clear the motorway and she would see the mountains, and home.

'Nick said he would retire to this,' she said when they had left Kendal behind.

'He'll be too old to climb then.'

'He feels it's his home. We might leave the house to him. Laurel would never want it.'

'What did you think of his partner?'

'Chris? They seemed eminently suited. I liked him. He and Nick are going to visit us next year.'

'Good. Are you calling him Nick now?'

'Yes, it seems to suit him. And me, now.'

They had plenty to talk about over supper, which Sam cooked. He had offered to take her out for a meal, but she refused. They wouldn't be able to talk easily with on-lookers. She felt glad to see him, and at the same time like a young girl. And on top of all that was the worry about his health.

'It was such a blow, Sam, when you told me about the biopsy,' she said. 'I wished I'd been with you.'

'So did I. Only you would have done. Alan says we should look in and see him.'

'OK. We'll do that.'

'I have to tell you that I missed you from the moment you left,' he said.

'I missed you, as if I'd lost an essential part of me.'

'Like Siamese twins?'

'Exactly.'

He asked if she minded a fry-up, and when she said no, he served up a heaped plateful of bacon, egg, mushrooms, peppers and tomatoes.

'Would you like some chips to go with that?' he asked. 'I've discovered how good they are out of a packet.'

'No, thanks! I have an elegant sufficiency here.' They laughed. 'Chris is a very good cook, you know. Nick sits back and leaves him to it.'

'Did you eat out at all?'

'Yes, we had lunch the day before I left. We had dim sum.'

'There's a place in Wetherham that does it. Perhaps we'll go sometime.'

'I would be afraid to. I prefer your fry-up. It's so English.'

'What's their pad like?'

'That's what it is. You remember how untidy Nick was? It's a spacious flat, in size rather like Laurel's, but hers is immaculate. She's becoming very American. She takes on the colour of her surroundings. Nick doesn't. But then Chris is English too. Very...'

'You got used to...it?'

'Yes, when you're with them, it seems the most natural thing in the world. Try not to worry, Sam. He and Laurel have chosen their paths. There's just you and me now. They're there to back us up if need be.'

'Yes, I accept that.'

'We've now got your problem to face.'

It was like honeymoon time again, Beth thought, or rather, the time when they had come back from their honeymoon and they were together, sanctified, playing at houses. They had both felt amused and surprised that they were allowed to go to bed together, and become known in the village as a married couple. For her to gradually get to know their neighbours, to entertain friends, mostly Sam's, to be someone with a decided status, was a revelation to her.

When Sam left for work, she would kiss him at the door, laughing inwardly at the stereotype they were enacting, and when he came back at night, she would welcome him in the same way, still feeling she was acting in a play. They had both been careful not to offend each other, either in thought, word or deed. She would never have let him see her slopping about in old comfortable clothes, wearing curlers – they had still felt they were on show to each other, and to the world, who they felt were observing this newly married couple.

No, it wasn't like that time, she decided on reflection. Only the shyness remained. Then they had been polite to each other, went to the loo secretly, dressed discreetly in the morning. The young of today didn't have that problem – that had all been taken care of before marriage.

But in bed now they felt able to talk freely about how they had missed each other. In retrospect it seemed much worse than it had been, and they both swore that it would never happen again. There was time for tenderness.

This idyll was broken, as it had to be, when Alan Barclay telephoned to say that Sam had to see the urologist at the hospital on the following Monday for the results.

They had been expecting it daily, but the news was a shock when it came. Alan asked them to call round that evening after surgery hours.

'Glad you're back, Beth,' Alan said. 'So Sam told you the news about his health?'

'Yes, I was with Nicholas in Hong Kong but flew back right away.'

'I'm glad you did. It's good to have someone who cares near you. Remember that time after the worry you had with Laurel in London, you came to see me? You had got quite depressed. I suggested you confide in Sam, and that he should take you away. People shouldn't bottle things up. The bottle explodes. But then you had the support of Sam.'

'I suppose every person is allowed one breakdown.' She felt Sam's eyes on her, but he didn't speak.

'But you did very well. That holiday seemed to set you up again.'

She decided to come clean. 'Not quite, Alan. I had depressive thoughts there.'

'Did you realize this, Sam?' And to her:

'But hadn't you finished the tablets I gave you?'

'No, I left off taking them when I was there. But I see now I was still depressed.'

'Why didn't you come to see me again?'

'I suppose depressives can't think straight. Don't let's pursue this, Alan. We're here about Sam.'

'Of course. But I warned you about suddenly stopping your medication. Now you have to remain strong and cheerful to support Sam.'

'I know. That's why I came home. Now, tell me what I need to know.'

'I advised him to get in touch with you, but he thought he knew best. You're both like naughty children. Well, as you probably know now, he's been through a series of tests. They thought it necessary for him to have a biopsy, which I'm sure he found pretty uncomfortable, eh?'

Sam shrugged. I should have been there, Beth thought, but then, he didn't tell me.

'Do you think it will be all right, Alan?' she asked.

'I wouldn't like to raise your hopes too

much. The urologist will have studied the pathologist's report, and will be anxious to tell you, hence this appointment on Monday. You'll go with him, Beth?'

'Sure. He won't be able to prevent me.' She looked at Sam. She could only guess how he was feeling, and castigated herself for not having been there for him.

'I'm hopeful for you, Sam. You've been fit all your life, and you're rather young for a bad result.' He got up. 'Must push on. Lilian gets mad at me for spoiling the supper she has so carefully produced. He shook hands with Sam and kissed Beth on the cheek. 'You haven't been to see us for far too long. And remember, Sam, you're quids in with Beth to support you.'

They spent the weekend walking in the Lakes, going to their favourite viewing places, their favourite pubs. Standing on Jenkins Crag and looking down Lake Windermere to Belle Isle, Beth said, 'This is what Nick misses. The space, water, land, sky.'

'And the heights,' Sam said. 'That

wonderful soaring feeling, like a bird, there's nothing to beat it.'

'Nor the satisfaction of a sandwich and tea from a flask, crouched under waterproofs in the rain.'

'We've had wonderful times with the children. Do you remember sliding down Langdale to the pub there for tea? And the glorious spread we got, with honey, strawberry jam, fresh butter, rum butter, an innumerable variety of scones on the table?'

'Marvellous! Wouldn't it be nice to do that again?'

'It would, but even if that pub's still there, you can't go back. We've had it.' She heard the ghostly voices of Laurel and Nick. 'Mum, he's hogging the strawberry jam.' And Nick, with a beatific smile, saying, 'Great grub!'

'But nothing can take away your memories. During our sailing days on the lake, my chief memories are of the wind and the rain on my face. And Nick and I falling in while tacking round the buoy. That's not something I would like to repeat.'

Each evening they ate in pubs they knew,

and although it was pleasant, Beth constantly thought, I'm living on the edge, and so is Sam. They didn't discuss the future.

The day came. They drove down the motorway to the hospital, where to their surprise they were shown into a room where they were told to wait. The urologist, Mr Beasley, would see them soon.

When the nurse went away, Beth said to Sam, 'Good news or bad news, let's think positively.' They sat in silence, side by side, and as he hadn't answered, she slipped her hand into his. 'OK, Sam?'

'Yes, thank you. I'm glad you're here.'

Mr Beasley bustled in, a short man, bald, but with a ready smile. 'Ah, Mr Crome,' he said and, looking at Beth, 'and this must be your wife? I'm pleased to meet you, Mrs Crome.' He extended a hand to her. He had the firm, positive grip of a man who had to deal with difficult problems.

He went round them and sat down at his desk, riffling through some papers. 'I won't keep you both in suspense. I'm pleased to tell you that I have the pathologist's report here,' he raised his head, 'and there's no sign of cancer.'

Sam's face lit up. He turned to Beth. 'Good news, eh?'

'Oh, yes,' she said. Relief flowed through her. She said to the urologist, 'You can imagine how worried we were. Thank you.'

'Don't thank me. Your husband has an excellent constitution, but sometimes that doesn't mean much. I, myself, thought he was too young, but one must go through the process. Luckily the result dispels any worries. I may say your husband has been an uncomplaining patient all along. I'm just as delighted as you are.'

'So what do I do now?' Sam asked.

'I should think a glass of champagne when you get home would be in order.' He smiled at them both. 'I shall be in touch with Dr Barclay, and he will give you instructions about check-ups.'

Their appointment had been in the morning, and when they got back, having stopped off at a motorway cafe, she said to Sam, 'Shall we have a celebratory dinner tonight with champagne? It's only twelve o'clock. I don't feel like anything to eat just now, how about you?'

'No, that stop on the motorway and their so-called quiche has quite put me off food for a long time. We'll have a slap-up meal at night, go out somewhere. Sharrow Bay?' He smiled at her. 'I don't seem to be able to settle. I think I'll go and work in the garden.'

'Good idea. I've got something to do there too.'

When she was in his garden shed with him, he took her in his arms. 'I feel we're in a new phase now. Both a little wiser, perhaps, but we'll make the most of our time together now.'

'Yes, there's nothing like a scare to make you feel blessed. At least that's how I feel.' She disengaged herself from his arms. 'In case you're feeling that I can't let you out of my sight, I really have a job in the garden which I've been promising myself to do. It's been at the back of my mind for some time.'

'What's that?'

'Have you got a stout pair of gloves? Thanks.' She took the gardening gloves he handed to her. 'I'm going to tackle the nettles growing round the compost bin. You can infuse them, I'm told, and make a good tea out of them, I can't remember the vitamin they contain. Or failing that, Mary Cass once told me young nettles can be used, in place of spinach, to make a quiche.' She looked at him, and saw he was embarrassed by the name.

'Good luck,' he said.

The strength necessary to pull the nettles out of the earth was just what she wanted. She worked hard, and soon she had a sizeable clump lying limply on the grass. She decided she would leave them there, and then get the barrow and pile them into it. She discovered she was weeping, the tears running down her hot face. She mopped it, but as fast as she mopped, they came faster. She gave up and took the path to the house. She passed the greenhouse where she saw Sam was busy with his tomatoes. He looked up and saw her, so she went through a pantomime of drinking tea. He nodded and she hurried into the house. In the kitchen, she flung water on her face, and mopped it with a towel, but still the tears came. She decided to make a job of it, and went into the sitting room where she sat down on the sofa, burying her face in the towel.

She had tidied herself up, fearful that Sam would come in and find her weeping, combed her hair and put on some lipstick, when the doorbell rang. When she answered it, Mary Cass was standing there. She looked quite shocked when Beth opened the door.

'Oh, Beth! I didn't know you were at home. You do look well! I came to see if there was anything I could do for Sam.'

You've done plenty, Beth thought, but should I ask her in?

'Sam's in the garden,' she said, trying to collect her wits.

'Is he? When did you get home, Beth?'

'Last week.'

'Oh! I was passing and thought I'd just look in and see if I...'

'Yes, you said that.'

'Has he had any results yet?'

'Yes, everything is all right. I went with him to the hospital today and he's got a clean bill of health.'

'Oh, that's marvellous!'

Sam appeared at Beth's side. 'Saw your car, Mary.' He looks worried, Beth thought, as well he may.

'Beth has just been telling me that you've got a clean bill of health. I'm so pleased for you. I called to see if there was anything I could do, but didn't expect to find Beth here.'

Beth thought, I'm watching a play here. Three characters, the old triangle. Looking at Mary, she remembered Nick's description of her, and anger seemed to burst through her chest. This fat slob had had the temerity to steal her husband! But you left him without giving a thought to Sam's welfare, she argued with herself. She was as much to blame in this triangle as Sam or Mary.

'Well, I'll push on,' Mary said.

'I've just been potting those plants you gave me,' Sam said. 'Thank you.'

'Oh, it was nothing. We've both got this interest in gardens,' she said to Beth.

'Yes, so you have.' Beth said. She looked at Mary, comments busily whirling about in her head. 'But gardens weren't your only

interest were they?' or 'You were quite prepared to have a fancy man around, but not
an invalid. You couldn't even share his worry
with him.' Selection was difficult.

'I got cleared this morning at the hospital,'
Sam said.

'Yes, so Beth had been telling me. Well, I
can't tell you how glad I am for both of you!'
She included them both in her benificent
smile.

Beth's anger had melted away, but she
proprietorially put her arm through Sam's
nevertheless. She returned Mary's smile.
This husband-stealer was actually her old
friend. She's alone, she hasn't her husband,
I have. 'Yes, it's good news. We're planning
ahead now,' she said.

Mary looked enquiringly at Sam. Beth
looked too. His face was tortured. She had
infinite sorrow for both of them, and some
for herself. This situation must prove something for all of them, like a play, she thought,
where it has all to be tied up at the end.

'Yes, the future seems quite clear to me
now,' Sam said, extracting his arm from
Beth's grasp to place it round her shoulder.

'I'd best be off,' Mary said.

'Has bridge started yet?' Beth asked, feeling sorry for her.

'Yes, Friday evening as usual.'

'We'll see you there, then. Goodbye.'

They waited until they saw Mary get into her car and drive away, then turned and went into the house. Sam sat down on the sofa and put his head in his hands. 'Cheer up, boyo,' Beth said. 'There were no recriminations. It will all be buried at the next bridge meeting.'

'Why on earth did she come back?'

'Credit her with kindness.' She sat down beside him and put her arm along his shoulders. 'I've never felt happier in my life, nor more humble. Give me a kiss.'

He turned towards her and said, 'You've been very generous, Beth.'

They kissed. 'I've suddenly got very clear sight. I think we've both found out that we need each other. Perhaps I had to go away to find this out,' she said.

'I wonder if I'll be blackballed at bridge on Friday,' Sam said.

They looked at each other and laughed.